SOME DREAM FOR FOOLS

BOOKS BY FAÏZA GUÈNE

Kiffe Kiffe Tomorrow

Some Dream for Fools

SOME DREAM FOR FOOLS

FAÏZA GUÈNE

Houghton Mifflin Harcourt

BOSTON • NEW YORK

2009

French © 2006 by Hachette Littératures
English translation © 2009 by Jenna Johnson

For information about permission to reproduce selections from this book,
write to Permissions, Houghton Mifflin Harcourt Publishing Company,
6277 Sea Harbor Drive, Orlando, Florida 32887-6777.

www.hmhbooks.com

Library of Congress Cataloging-in-Publication Data
Guène, Faïza.
[Du rêve pour les oufs. English]
Some dream for fools / Faïza Guène.
p.   cm.
ISBN 978-0-15-101420-0
1. Immigrants—France—Fiction. 2. Family—France—Fiction.
3. Family—Algeria—Fiction. 4. France—Social conditions—Fiction.
5. Algeria—Social conditions—Fiction. I. Title.
PQ3989.3.G84D813 2009
843'.912—dc22   2008050167

Book design by Brian Moore

Printed in the United States of America

DOC 10 9 8 7 6 5 4 3 2 1

For my family.
My father, Abdelhamid Guène.
My mother, Khadra Kadri.
My sister, Mounia Guène.
My brother, Mohamed Guène.
That you may be proud of me.
I love you.

For all those who have supported and encouraged me.
For the Courtillières, represent.
For my friends, thank you.
For those who have been imprisoned, stay strong.
For Algeria.
For all the crazy fools, here and over there.
For those who dream.

GLOSSARY

aâmi — my uncle; an honorific for a male elder

bakchich — tip, bribe

belâani — to pretend

bendirs — North African percussion instrument

bled — (1) a village; (2) a godforsaken place, the middle of nowhere, a wasteland; (3) a hole or dump; (4) countryside, terrain; (5) the interior of North Africa, the Maghreb (French, by way of Algerian Arabic *blad*)

bledard — a person from the *bled*

boléta — ball

châab — people; here, the North African people living in North Africa

chabin — Creole term for a person of mixed racial heritage or a person of Afro-Caribbean heritage with light skin; here, used in its feminine form, **chabines** (Caribbean, specifically the Antilles)

chétane — devil

djellabas — a loose-fitting outer robe

djoufs — here, girls whose heritage links them to parts of Africa that contain El Djouf, a region of sand dunes that is part of the Sahara. Countries containing or touching El Djouf include Mauritania, Algeria, Morocco, and Mali. El Djouf means "empty place."

el aïn — the evil eye

franssaouis — French

frotti-frotta — close, sensual dancing

gandouras — sleeveless, light dresses of Berber origin, worn in North Africa, often around the house

habs — prison

haik — traditional outfit consisting of a piece of light-colored fabric which women roll or drape around the entire body

hanout — store

inchallah — var. *inshallah*; literally, "if Allah wills"; God willing

istiqlal — independence

khoyya — brother; also a general term for a male friend or relative

kiffe — to be really crazy about something

kou yinkaranto — idiots (Sonninké)

labès — part of a traditional Muslim greeting, roughly, "How are you?"

miskina—the poor

miskine—poor guy; an expression of pity

naâl chétane—Curse the devil!

sadaqa—offering

salaam—the "hello" portion of the ceremonial Muslim greeting, often accompanied by a bow with the right palm placed on the forehead

starfoullah—May God preserve us!

toubab—a white person, particularly used in African countries to refer to white Europeans, somewhat pejorative (etymology uncertain, but probably from Wolof)

verlan—slang for *à l'envers*, literally, "inside out" or "back to front"; the name of a type of French slang that involves reordering syllables in a word or phrase

youyous—ululations

ziara—a disenchantment, the breaking of a spell

SOME DREAM FOR FOOLS

Big City Cold

IT'S FREEZING IN THIS *bled,* the wind makes my eyes water and I have to run in place to get warm. I tell myself that I'm not living in the right place, that the climate around here isn't for me, because in the end, climate's the only thing that counts and this morning the crazy French cold paralyzes me.

My name is Ahlème and I roam around in the middle of everybody, the ones who run, the ones who beat each other up, are late, argue, make phone calls, the ones who don't smile, and I see my brothers who, like me, are very cold. I always recognize them, they have something in their eyes that isn't the same as everybody else, like they want to be invisible, or be somewhere else. But they're here.

1

At home, I don't complain, even when they cut off the heat, or else Papa tells me: "Don't even talk, you weren't here for the winter of '63." I don't answer him, in '63 I wasn't even born. So I head out and wander around the wonderfully smooth streets of France, I pass rue Joubert where some hookers yell across the street to each other. You could say that these old, wrecked dolls aren't afraid of the cold anymore. Prostitutes are the climatic exception, location doesn't matter, they don't feel anything anymore.

My appointment at the temp agency is at 10:40. Not 10:45. Not 10:30. Everything's precise in France, every minute counts and I can't seem to make myself get into the rhythm. I was born on the other side of the sea and the African minute has more than sixty seconds.

On the instructions of M. Miloudi, the adviser at my neighborhood unemployment office, I went to talk to this new place: Interim Plus.

Miloudi, he's a real veteran. He's been at the agency for the Insurrection Housing Projects for years and must have seen through every case in the district. He's pretty efficient. But he's also always in a hurry. At my interview, he didn't waste a minute:

"Sit down, young lady . . ."

"Thank you, sir."

"And next time, mind that you knock before you come in, please."

"Sorry, sir, I didn't think about it."

"I'm telling you for your own good, because that sort of thing could cost you an interview."

"I'll remember."

"Good, so let's get started, no wasting time, we only have twenty minutes ahead of us. You are going to fill out the competency form in front of you, write in the boxes in capital letters and don't make any spelling mistakes. If there's a word that makes you hesitate, ask me for the dictionary. You brought your résumé?"

"Yes. Five copies, like you said."

"Very good. Here's the paper, fill it out carefully. I'll be back in five minutes."

He took a box of kitchen matches and his pack of Marlboros out of his pocket then left the room, leaving me to stare down my destiny. On the desk there were piles of folders, a mess of papers that blocked your sight, they took up all the space on the desk. And above it all, an enormous clock hung on the wall. Every tick of its hands knocked out a sound that reverberated in me as if it were my death knell. All of a sudden I was hot. I was blocked. The five minutes passed like a high-speed train and I hadn't written anything but my last name, my first name, and my date of birth.

I heard M. Miloudi's hacking cough in the hallway, he came back into the room.

"So? Where are you? Have you finished?"

"No, I'm not done."

"But you haven't filled out anything!" he said as he leaned over the paper.

"I haven't had enough time."

"There are lots of people who are waiting for appointments, I have to see other people after you, you saw them in the waiting room. We only have ten minutes left at the most to contact the SREP, because it won't help at all to go through the AGPA at this time of year, there aren't any more spots. We can try FAJ, the paid apprenticeship program . . . Why haven't you filled it out yet? It's pretty simple."

"I don't know what to put in the box marked 'life objective'—"

"Do you have any ideas?"

"No."

"But on your résumé, it's clear that you have a lot of work experience, there has to be something that you liked in all of that."

"I've only had little jobs as a waitress or salesperson. Just to make money, sir, not as part of my life objective."

"Fine, let's forget the form, we don't have time. I'm going to give you the address of our temp agency so you can go while we're waiting to contact FAJ."

Johanna, an office worker at Interim Plus, looks about sixteen, has a quivering voice, and speaks like every word hurts her. I realize she's asking me to fill out a questionnaire; she gives me a pen with their ridiculous office logo on it and tells me to follow her. The mademoiselle is wearing ultra-tight jeans that betray every violation of her Weight Watchers diet and give her the look of an adulterous woman. She points me toward a chair near a small table where I can settle in. I have trouble writing, my fingers are frozen, I struggle to loosen them. It reminds me of when Papa—The Boss, as we call him—used to get home from work. He always needed a little time to open his hands. "It's from the jackhammer," he said.

I scratch along, I fill out their boxes, I check things off, I sign my name. Everything is miniscule on their form and their questions are kind of annoying. No, I am not married, I don't have children, I am not a B-permit cardholder, I haven't done any higher education, I am not a Cotorep-verified disabled person, I am not French. Where do I find the box marked "My life is a complete failure"? At least with that I could just immediately check yes, and we wouldn't have to talk about anything else.

In a compassionate tone, Johanna, her jeans pulled so tight they could make her uterus explode, presents my first "interim mission." It's funny that they call them missions. It makes these shitty jobs feel like adventures.

She offers me a stock job at Leroy Merlin next Friday evening. I say yes without the smallest hesitation, I really need to work and I would take pretty much anything.

I leave the office all satisfied, proof it doesn't take much.

Later I head out to meet Linda and Nawel at La Cour de Rome, a bar near the agency over in Saint-Lazare. They've been trying to see me for a few weeks and I admit I dodge going out when I'm broke. And then the last few times, the girls have all been glued to their boyfriends and it wears me out, always feeling uncomfortable planted there alone in the middle of them. I'm not far from winning the Third-Wheel Championship title for all Europe and Africa.

The girls are set up in a banquette at the back of the room. I knew it, they're always like that, I know their old secret smoker tricks by heart. Back in the neighborhood, they even have their own headquarters. They're always fucking around behind the stadium, lighting one up. Their secret phrase for meeting up is: "Let's go play some sports."

As usual, they're all tricked out. I notice that they're always classed up and I wonder how they ever find enough time to get dressed, put on makeup, do their hair. Nothing is left to chance, everything matches, is calculated, chosen with care.

The few times I agree to make this kind of effort, it really takes it out of me, it's too much work. What won't we chicks do to draw just one nice look or a compliment in our days racked with doubt. And the ones who say that they do themselves all up like this just for their own pleasure, yeah, my eye!

When I get to the girls, they light their cigarettes in perfect unison and welcome me with a warm, smoky hello.

Just to keep things on script, this is followed by a "What's new?" with a few seconds' pause afterward to think about an answer before they jump right back into their conversation.

Then comes the inevitable question I always dread.

"And how're things with the boys?" A quick shake of the head does the trick. They understand right away. I wonder why, whenever they ask this question, they make "boy" plural. It's hard enough to find one love, why make things even more complicated?

Then, like always, the eternal refrain: "How can a pretty girl like you still be single? It's because you don't really want it . . . It's your fault, you're too difficult . . . We've introduced you to a whole mess of guys, from the beasts to the super-slick, there's nothing more we can do for you, you're all closed up."

I can't seem to make them understand that my life isn't as bad as they think, because if everything goes well menopause isn't going to come tomorrow. But there's nothing I can do, they're just going to keep hitting me with losers.

Guys with an IQ of 2, who talk themselves up to no end, all pretentious, guys who are incapable of conversation or who are chronically depressed.

So I manage a magnificent sidestep anyone would be proud of and change the subject—this is my real talent, I'm triple champion of all Africa and Europe at jumping over obstacles and problems.

Actually I think that, like most people, they already have their lives planned out in their heads, all the elements are there, like pieces of a puzzle that are just waiting to be put together. They split their time between work and play, go on vacation to the same place every summer, always buy the same brand of deodorant, have cool families and boyfriends that they have been with forever. Even their boys are "no-fault" guys, the kind I like but would never personally go away with for a weekend. Not one false note. They all come from the same village as the girls, back in the *bled*, so that's going to please their parents. You might say that we're living out a sort of return to incest. At least with your brother, you can be sure that he comes from exactly the same place as you, you can verify it, ask your mother. The girls find this very practical, because if your traditions are different, your families don't agree about everything; and then it's complicated when you're teaching your kids, when you're not even speaking the same language . . . Me, I say that these are just ridiculous details, and you shouldn't build a home on such practical questions.

Nawel just came back from vacation, she was in Algeria with her father's family, and I mentioned that she lost lots of weight, at least ten pounds.

"Oh yeah? I really got skinny?"

"You're practically dried up. I almost feel sorry for you, *miskina*."

"It's the back-to-the-*bled* effect."

"The vacation diet, right?"

"Yeah, that's right. . . . The heat, the stuffed green beans at every meal, your grandmother's jokes, those Chilean soap operas. . . . Of course you lose weight."

"But how did you make it? Two months is plenty in the *bled*, I would have been completely depressed . . ." I asked Nawel, intrigued.

"Eh, it just passes. The only thing that was a little harsh was that on the TV there was only one channel. Even *Mr. Bean* is censored there."

"At least that means you don't have to put up with that annoying moment when the whole group is in front of the TV and BAM! there's a hot sex scene or an ad for douche. Then, the dad starts coughing and you have to be quick, take the remote, and shut that thing right off. This is why now, at my house, we have a satellite dish. It saves us all the time because on French television they love to put naked women all over the screen at the drop of a hat."

"And things were good with your family?"

"My cheap-ass family . . . The first week they loved us because the suitcases were packed full. As soon as we passed out all the gifts, it was over, we didn't rate with them at all. I told my mother: 'Next summer, I swear on the Koran, we'd better ask that discount store Tati to be our corporate sponsor.'"

Later it's time to catch up on the neighborhood gossip with Linda.com. She's a force of nature, a true talker. Linda, she knows what's happening with everyone, I don't know how she does it, sometimes she even knows people's stories before they know themselves.

"Do you know Tony Lopez?"

"No, who is he?"

"Come on, he's the new guy on sixteen."

"The blond?"

"No, the tall brunet. He works at Midas."

"Yeah, and what about him?"

"He's going out with Gwendoline!"

"The little one? The redhead in your building?"

"No, not her. The anorexic, the one who's covered with unfinished tattoos. Nawel, you have to know who she is."

"Yeah, I know the one, I see her on the bus every time I go to work. Hey maybe you know something that's always intrigued me, do you know why she's never finished one of her tattoos?"

"How is she supposed to know that?" I said naively.

"No, no, I know—"

"Fuck, you freak me out, you're a real professional gossip you know? Tell us."

"She was with this really shady guy before, a tattoo artist. And that's it. He started all these tattoos on her and he never finished them before he dumped her for another girl."

"A true bastard. He could have at least finished the job."

"Okay, so the anorexic is going out with Tony Lopez, and what else?"

"And he wanted to break up with her. According to my sources, it's because he was messing around with the accountant at Midas. And Gwendoline was so crazy for him, she gave him all this psychological pressure to stay with her. So he ended up staying with her but he made her pay . . ."

"What? Spill! Stop stringing us along."

"She's knocked up, the little thing. Pregnant up to her eyeballs. Crazy right?"

And there you go, every time she ends with "Crazy right?"

She told us two or three stories that had to be whispered before she left us with a smile that made everyone wonder what our secrets were and that shields me from the outside world and its cold.

The platform is black with the crowds, there are service disruptions on the line. One train in four, I think, at least that's what they said on the radio.

So I'm forced up against the pole in this car. There's no air in the RER, everyone's pushing me, blocking me in. The train sweats and me, I feel smothered by all these sad silhouettes, all looking for a little color. You could say that all the air in Africa wouldn't be enough. They're phantoms, they're sick, contaminated by sadness.

Me, I'm going back to Ivry to see my neighbor, Auntie Mariatou, and her children. My asthmatic RER will cough me up in my zone where it's even colder. There are some days like that where you don't know anymore where you're going, you feel like you don't have any luck at all, and that's just too bad. It's true that it's sad, but fortunately, at the end, there's always this little thing that gets us up in the morning. No guarantee, but you think that one day, one day it will be better. Like Auntie says: "The most beautiful stories are the ones that start badly."

The Dollar Tree

I ENVY THE KIDS in this house. It's beautiful the way that they are surrounded by love and warmth, this family is a true poem. Auntie Mariatou is motherhood in all its splendor, so soft you might even say she was made of cotton itself—the better to wrap her little ones snug. I'm fascinated every time to see her teach them so firmly but always dripping with honey. When I talk about her I get a little carried away, it's true, but this is the woman I want to become some day. For me she is a model, all at once a woman, a mother, and a wife. Auntie is very beautiful, her lips are full, her hips broad, and her curves fed the dreams of more than one man in the village back in the day. And though she's a plump woman, she does have something in her that makes her naturally walk as light as an antelope. A certain je ne sais quoi, as the French would say, that would make those 60-pound mannequins tremble.

She and her husband, Papa Demba, have made four beautiful children who came one right after the other and resemble one another just like Russian dolls. The oldest is called Wandé, and she's eight years old. Today I came over to help her do her homework. She dreams of becoming a singer and complains that no *toubab* in her class wants to be her boyfriend because she has fake hair. Then come Issa and Moussa, the twins. They are too mischievous these two, and they scare me the way they will believe anything anyone says. As for the last one, he only knows how to scream for now—he's barely six months old. He's my pride and joy, the little one. It was me who whispered his baptismal name to Auntie Mariatou when she was at the end of her pregnancy and running out of ideas. I chose Amady because it's the name of the first boy I ever loved. I remember being so crazy about him. He would always play with me on the merry-go-round and push with all his strength. I would go so fast that my little pleated skirt would rise without anything to stop it because my hands would be glued to the bars. I was always too afraid of falling on my face to ever let go of them.

That devil Amady regularly used this little strategy in order to get a peek under my skirt. I didn't understand it until a long time afterward because I was only five years old at the time.

Anyway back to the subject of baby Amady. While Auntie was walking him in his stroller around the big park, she was stopped by the old Gypsy woman, the one everybody thinks is crazy. And she told her that this baby would one day become an exceptional man who was going to change history forever, that he would do something very great and that it would take everyone by surprise. She said that the baby carried the promise of an entire people in his belly.

Of course, like most of the people here Auntie Mariatou didn't take her seriously. She even laughed when she thought about it again later as she changed her son's diaper.

"If all the promise that this little one carries in his belly turns into crap, then those people are up shit's creek, no?"

Even if everyone says that she's crazy and just scares the children, me, I find the old Gypsy very interesting. From time to time I get to observe her from a distance, just as she is. In the morning, she takes herself for a walk, she marches along, her shoulders covered by a big black shawl, and stops sometimes to feed the birds. And honestly, deep down, she gives me the heebie-jeebies, especially when I see her talking to the pigeons. She tricks one of them, always the fattest. Then she puts the bird in her hand, and it's bizarre, because every time he stays calm, he doesn't even try to fly away. Then she begins murmuring things to him. From far away you might think that the bird answers her and that they settle in for a discussion, all natural. This lasts a little while and then, all of a sudden, she lets out a horrible, high-pitched scream and all the birds that she has invited to her bread-crumb party let fly in every direction. They take off like maniacs. It's anarchy in the gray Ivry sky.

When everything quiets down, the beating of wings a little farther off, you notice something very strange. The old woman is still there, standing, stiff as a stick, and in the hollow of her hand, up near her mouth, the fat pigeon stays peaceful. Usually, in the end, she leaves with the bird as if nothing happened, and gradually, the greedy little pigeons wait for the old lady to depart to come back one by one to get a little dessert.

Sometimes I imagine the after-party: she twists the bird's neck and crunches into it, sinking her canine teeth into it like a starving she-wolf. Then she finishes by swallowing the whole thing raw, feathers, head, beak, and all.

This old lady truly intrigues me. I wouldn't know what age she could be, or what era she's from either. It's like she exists outside of time.

I am sitting on a wooden chair in the middle of the room and waiting impatiently for the nightly episode of *Star Academy* to end so I can finally start working with Wandé. Impossible to get her to leave her post, she's stuck to it like a cockroach on a Raid strip. I think it's because she's in love with one of the contestants, the little blond who's made it to the finals. She makes me think of my little brother, Foued, when he's in front of the PlayStation playing his war games.

"Wandé! It's already seven-thirty, my love! I'm not going to wait all night for your homework."

"But it's the finals."

15

"I'm warning you—after this I'm going back to my house. Either you turn off the TV now, or you do your homework all by yourself."

"Let it go, Ahlème. She's just going to get a zero."

"Mama, shh! I can't hear anything!"

"What! Who did you tell to shh? Were you raised so badly?"

"It's because she's on a date with her future husband. He's going to sing," I said, trying to tease Wandé.

Auntie Mariatou, furious, ripped out the TV plug.

"Still, there are some things more important than television! This kid would rather piss all over herself than miss a second of this show, it's terrible."

Wandé starts to get angry and takes on this sulky air that she does so well.

Since she had her first braids, she gets such a funny puss when she sulks. Her face is all tight, pulled to the back. Cornrows are the African face-lift. Auntie Mariatou always pulls too tight. I know, she's done my hair too. The result is right pretty but, in order to achieve it, she pulls at your head like it's a carpet and this can last for hours. If you grit your teeth it goes a little better. At the same time, she knows what she's doing, it's her career and you should never correct someone who's working, that's what The Boss says. There are clients who come from far away for Auntie to do their hair because she has a steady hand and really knows what's in style, what will make them happy, and what will work for them.

Recently she started subscribing to an American magazine

on Afro hairdressing. She says that black women in America are fearless with their hair, they're likely to try the craziest things. In this magazine, they tell the secrets of the stars—like Mary J. Blige or Alicia Keys for example.

Auntie's funny when she talks about that, she gets all carried away.

"What do you think? This girl here, Beyoncé, the one who waddles around in those clips on MTV, you think she was born with blond hair as smooth as silk? The truth is that her hair is as frizzy as mine, my dear, except that she, she has the means to make everyone forget it, that's all."

Auntie Mariatou works four days a week at Afro Star 2000, a salon in Paris, in the Château-d'Eau neighborhood. Of all the heads she works on, mostly people from the Ivory Coast, many of them have become good friends.

Auntie loves doing hair and has had a passion for it for a long time. Her secret dream is to move over there, to America, and open a big salon.

"Big deal if I don't speak English, I will use the language of hair itself."

Her dream of America goes back to her childhood. She too had a face drawn tight from the back by the braids her mother gave her. And while everyone had nothing but Paris on their lips, she saw only New York. Sometimes she says that if she hadn't followed love and her husband, Papa Demba, to France, she would certainly have gone over there to join I don't know which distant cousin.

17

When Auntie Mariatou lived in Senegal, in Mbacké, whenever the time for the American soap operas would come, every neighborhood would gather in front of a little television installed in the middle of the courtyard. It was practically a religious ritual. Whenever it was super-bright and sunny out, someone would get up and put a palm leaf above the screen.

Sometimes the image would get scrambled or the worn-out set would even stop showing anything for a minute or two. An eternity for the little girl who had tears in her eyes and started cursing everything she could until one of the other viewers would get up and repair the receiver. Often it was her cousin Yahia, the one who was nicknamed Romeo in the village because he courted all the girls behind their parents' backs. He would go find a nice stainless-steel fork that he would plant in the ass of the temperamental TV. What's more, that same fork had, incidentally, served several days before to stem little Aminata's tetanus spasms.

It always happened that this D-list method worked very well and quickly enough would have its effect: the image returned in less time than it would take to say so and the entire assembly would cry out an "aaah" of relief. Mariatou always arranged to put herself in the front row so she had the best seat. Mouth wide open, fascinated by what she saw, she was so focused that she didn't even take the trouble to shoo the flies that came and landed on her face or that tickled her naked, dry feet.

Her cousin Yahia, alias Romeo, the one with the fork in the TV, amused by the fascination this little girl had for the big world on the other side of the ocean, fed her a line just to have a little fun with her. He told her a story that she believed in as hard as iron: The Legend of the Dollar Tree.

"This legend says that in America there are extraordinary trees. These magic trees produce bills for leaves, dollar bills. These trees thrive under any conditions, they don't need water because they water themselves, and they're in bloom all year long. Everyone has the right to profit from these trees, and it's for this reason that these people know neither hunger nor thirst."

Mariatou dreamed of the dollar tree from morning to night until she reached the age of reason.

I think she still believes in it a little and that we've all believed in it once. The Boss, he was convinced that in France all you had to do was dig into the soil to make your fortune. When he told us that, it hurt my heart but I smiled all the same.

Dignified and Standing Tall

"YOU OKAY, PAPA?"

"It's cold here. You know, I only have five cigarettes to last the whole rest of the evening."

"That's because they cut off the heat, I told you that yesterday, they're going to turn it back on in a week. And I'll go buy some more cigarettes at the store, they close late."

"Weren't you just out?"

"I was out since this morning."

"Oh, okay. I didn't hear you leave."

"By the way, Papa, do you keep up with Michel, our upstairs neighbor?"

"The one missing an arm?"

"No, the other one."

"Which other one? The skinny guy who's always fighting with his wife, the one who's as nasty as anyone?"

"No, the fat one with the glasses, the same one whose dog died last year."

"What about him?"

"It sounds like he tried to commit suicide."

"Again?"

"Yeah, it's the third time . . . no, the fourth, I think."

"Four times already? My God, that happened fast. And did he die?"

"No, he failed again, he's in the hospital."

"You see, I always told you he was a failure, that one. Couldn't even kill himself! It's not all that hard, dying."

"Yeah, sure."

"You know, I only have five cigarettes for—"

"Yeah, I know, I'm going down to find some. Where's Foued, Papa?"

"He's playing ball outside with the kids."

"Good, I'm going to find him, he should be home by this hour, and you know it, it's ten-thirty—"

"Ten-thirty? It's late, the smoke shop is going to close . . ."

The Boss, he's always like that, but lately I have the feeling it's getting worse. He's been like this ever since the accident, which will be three years next month. Three years, it's not a huge deal, but to see him in this state, in the middle of sentences that don't make any sense, sitting all day in his armchair, in pajamas, you

21

might think he had always been there. So he spends all his time in front of the TV, which has become a member of the family in its own right. It's the TV that regulates The Boss's new life, he doesn't need a watch anymore. *Morning TV,* that's time for coffee, news, and breakfast; *Derrick,* that's when he takes his nap; and the last shot from the evening movie, that's when he goes to bed. Since he went off the rails, he lives a never-ending day.

I remember, it happened very early in the morning, he was working at the building site and he was keeping his balance up there, like he had kept his balance his whole life.

Only that day, he wasn't wearing his helmet. Papa had given his to Fernandes — the one who never drank — because he was walking under the girders and Papa thought it was dangerous. If I know him, The Boss must have said: "Me, I'm all the way up here, so I'm not in danger of anything falling on my head except maybe lightning."

No one knows exactly why he fell from that bitch of a beam. The fall was so spectacular that all the boys thought he was done for. The truth is that his body didn't suffer anything truly horrible, two or three broken ribs and a ridiculous ankle sprain.

Only, as he fell over, his head hit a joist and because of the blow it doesn't turn all the way around anymore.

He wasn't wearing his helmet, so the boss refused to pay him damages. There was first the workers union, and then the lawsuit, the lawyer, the trial. Luckily he won the case in the end. Recognized disability, incapable of working. So he gets a pension and even a free transit card.

But I remember that with the lawyer we really had to do battle by shuffling papers in every sense, doctors' affidavits, declarations of one sort or another.

It's true that it was hard at first but afterward we managed.

During the first months following the accident, there were mornings when Papa woke up at 4:00, in the middle of the week, like usual, went through his ablutions, prayed, made his lunch, and dressed himself to go out. It seems to me he wasn't doing all this in a logical order anyway. When I realized that he was standing, I had to get myself up and explain to him that he wasn't going to work and it broke my heart because he answered me, confused: "Yes, it's true, you're right, I forget, it's Sunday."

Foued really doesn't like it that I go looking for him when he's outside with his buddies, he says that I embarrass him—he's Mr. Big, you understand. In general, I avoid it, it's true, but this time I warned him and noted that he doesn't really care about disrespecting the rules I make for the house. After all, he's a kid, he's only fifteen. He has to get up early to go to school tomorrow morning, and there's nothing for him to be doing outside at this hour.

He's probably at the other end of the neighborhood, at the Pierre de Coubertin Stadium. I've noticed that most of the sports fields are named after Pierre de Coubertin. What a lack of originality! Me, I propose that one day we rebaptize our stadium Ladji Doucouré.

Anyway, the stadium is at the foot of what everyone calls "The Hill," a sort of big rise that hangs over the whole neighborhood. I position myself at this strategic spot, and there an extraordinary view lies waiting. Lights come toward me from every side and it's so beautiful to me.

I am surrounded by all these buildings with all their crazy sides that hold in our noises, our odors, our lives here. I stand there, alone, in the middle of their strange architecture, their gaudy colors, their unconscious forms that have cradled our illusions for so long. The time has passed when running water and electricity were enough to camouflage injustices, the slums are far off now. I am dignified and standing tall and I'm thinking about a whole mess of things. The events that took place in our neighborhood during these last few weeks have stirred up the press around the world, and after some face-offs between the police and the kids, everything is newly settled down. But what can our three burned-out cars change when an army of maniacs are trying to make us shut up?

The only curfew worth minding is the one I, non-French citizen, will impose this evening on my fifteen-year-old brother.

I see Foued down below, right in the middle of the stadium, running around, agile, he's easy to recognize. He's playing with about ten other neighborhood boys around the same age. For the most part I know them, I've watched some of them grow up. I can see that even the Villovitch brothers are here. I haven't run into these two hooligans in an eternity. They've been avoiding me since our last encounter. They must have been so ashamed that they would willingly clear away like the fog if they could.

That night I had gone down to the basement to lock up Foued's bike. I opened the bulletproof door, which got jammed a little as I pushed the front wheel, and it was there that I took those two scoundrels by surprise. They were planted on this old two-seater couch that's been in retirement in the basement for years, and since they had their backs to me, they didn't immediately see my intrusion on their privacy.

Right in front of me, I discovered the ingenious contraption they had cooked up. Thanks to a pirated outlet, they had installed a little television, placed it on an upside-down cardboard box, and below it a game console served as their DVD player. It was some comic scene, I just saw what was happening on the couch, which was basically their little clammy necks and their right arms jiggling nervously.

At the heart of this little staging, an official episode of the Young Olympics was playing. On the TV, a busty blond bimbo was carrying out a perilous performance of rhythmic gymnastics, supported a little too closely by these guys on the parallel bars. The basement had been transformed into a screening room of Cinema Blonde-Trash.

O Puberty I write your name.
On Concrete, I write your name.

At this fateful moment, I decided not to laugh. I didn't want to take the risk of castrating these virile budding men and having the responsibility for all their future troubles. Then came the inevitable "ahem"—I had to interrupt this sketch in order to put the bike away.

I will never forget the expression on their faces. They were caught red-handed, with no desire to play any awkward word games. I did serious violence to myself to lock down and keep my cool, using sadness to fight back this irresistible need to laugh that was pestering me.

The villains didn't dare turn their heads in my direction, they put away their hardware, feverish with shame. I got out of that basement à la Ali Baba and His Forty Tools, leaving those two foxes with their remorse so I could finally let my wild laughter shake itself out on the elevator. I nearly went back down to thank them, it had been such a long time since I had laughed so wholeheartedly. And there it is, that's why they avoid me, those two disgusting little creeps.

I make my way onto the field and already my little Zizou-in-training is blasting me a look. He wants my hide for coming into his territory.

And respect for elders? I'm going to take him back to the house by the elastic in his underwear if I have to. Who does he think he is? I raised him, this kid, and even if his memory is short, I remember very well. He owes me obedience. Now that he's terminated his contract with Pampers he thinks he doesn't owe me any respect. That's the best shit yet.

"Foued! Come home right now!"

"One last little game and I'll be there. Go ahead, it's all right."

"This isn't a discussion. Let's go," I said.

"It's fine, okay! You're boring the shit out of me. I'll be home afterward."

"Shut up! Listen to how you talk to me! You want to act like the big man in front of your boys, yeah, well, you failed at that my old man. Get over here!"

He quits his leg tricks, ultra-pissed, and stays put. Suddenly there's a silence in the group. We're about sixty feet from each other, we're both standing straight up, and so begins a great battle of looks. It was like a Western of the this-town-isn't-big-enough-for-both-of-us variety.

To my great shock, at this critical point in the movie, one of the Villovitch brothers had the balls to speak up.

"Let him play one more game, please, it's not right!"

"You, little shit, no one asked you anything as far as I know. It's not your place to tell me what is or isn't right . . ."

Mr. Mini-glans lowers his head, humiliated. I confess, I hit him a little hard. But at the same time the dirty kids wanted to usurp power. I was the victim of a coup d'état, so I had to be firm.

Foued follows me without saying anything, he's even too ashamed to say goodbye to his friends. If at this exact moment he had a gun in place of his eyes, I bet he would have already put a bullet in my back. I don't need to talk either, I know that he knows. Papa should never be alone in the house, that's rule number one. Sometimes I get the feeling that I was born to take care of other people. Foued is young, he isn't responsible for all of it, but he needs to understand that he can't just do what he wants. He's at the age where you start to build—and not on construction sites, like The Boss, who spent his whole life earning practically no francs an hour, coming home dirty and exhausted, hands ruined and back broken with the strain. I would be thrilled to read a little motivation on Foued's face when he decides to do his homework. This pisser never does shit.

The Cat with Nine Lives

FROM NOW ON, I'll think twice before using the expression "That's not even worth a nail." Today I know better than anyone the exact value of a nail, this little object that seems without importance at first but which is in reality the source of all things. We don't think about them enough.

The night before my stock job started, I got a phone call from that dear Johanna, the girl from my temp agency. It's already an accomplishment to understand what she's talking about when you're in front of her, but on the phone it's practically a miracle. You almost want to give her speech therapy for her birthday.

So she called me to give me instructions for the "inventory" mission.

"Be a volunteer, be motivated, show your supervisor that you deserve the opportunity that you've been given in being hired, wear the employment agency's name with conviction."

Of course they don't send just anyone to their client businesses. Especially to spend an evening counting nails in an empty store.

I arrived at Leroy Merlin very early—I always do that just to be sure. Punctuality is like a sickness for me. I don't like people who always arrive late, especially the ones who don't think it's a big deal. When someone makes me wait a long time, I take off and that's that. The Boss often says: "If you wait for someone once, you'll be waiting for him your whole life."

Once on the premises, I had to talk to a certain Sonia, a thin, dry woman around thirty years old.

When the crew was finally at the meeting spot, she turned to explaining how our crazy evening would unfold.

One break—pee or cigarette—for a maximum of ten minutes, so it's impossible to smoke and piss, you have to choose, unless you do both at the same time. Then a formal prohibition against leaving the store with your bag or jacket during inventory. What are they afraid of? That someone will discreetly steal a sink?

So all the people are for the most part in their twenties, the majority are students, and it's a group composed mostly of boys.

Sonia assigns us to departments with partners.

With my luck, I end up in the hardware department with a little guy named Raphaël Vignon who didn't leak a single word the whole evening. Wonderful! There I am stuck in the festival of nails, screws, and bolts with a kid suffering from verbal constipation. Sometimes I feel his disturbing gaze on me, but I continue to count my nails as if nothing is happening, even though really I am a little creeped out—empty stores, like underground parking garages, call to mind murder scenes. At certain points in the evening, I nearly forgot he was there, but at that exact moment he starts whistling or hacking out a cough or something like that.

What a life! I could have ended up with another partner, the big brunet in the back for example, the cute one with the good body who I saw giving me little interested glances. But no, I had to be inflicted with this Vignon, with his domestic-animal-assassin demeanor. It's always like this anyway, I don't know why I'm still surprised to find myself in these kinds of situations. It's my destiny, I should get used to it.

Plus my back and my legs hurt. In the process of becoming glued to the stepladder, I had these ugly marks on both of my knees, and all for a payoff of 65 euros. With this pile of cash I can only go to the market twice.

I think I've been stuck with the stupidest little jobs imaginable. Except for maybe playing Santa Claus at the Galeries Lafayette.

I was a counselor for little kids at a vacation camp. I know all about pissed-in pants, untied shoelaces, boogers hanging out of noses, tantrums and fits of tears. And being paid in peanuts of course.

I've passed out balloons shaped like hearts on Valentine's Day at the Thiais shopping mall. I met the most wild-in-love couples in the entire Val-de-Marne that day, I remember, and it hit me hard because I'd been dumped the night before.

Then there was the wave of stints in restaurant work, McDonald's, Quick, Paul, KFC. I remember gaining at least five pounds that I lost right away when I was a waitress at the Nut House, the bar that makes you nuts.

I even worked for a phone chat line. It paid well and I worked under the charming pseudonym Samantha. I cracked quick enough though because it was too shady. I put a stop to it the night that a guy, one who called pretty regularly, asked me to imitate a hen.

I also went door-to-door selling prepaid cell phones. I can't count the times someone slammed the door in my face screaming: "I don't believe in God, I'm not interested."

Before that, I worked for a telemarketing company that sold surveillance cameras. We pulled our numbers primarily from stores in the super-luxe sixteenth, eighth, and seventh arrondissements. Every morning a guy the employees nicknamed Cocaine came to brief us in the office. He tried to put little disks in our heads, like: "You're winners, believe it! Today will be great!" And of course he always slid in there that the one who sold the most should get a bonus of half their salary. I was fired at the end of a week because I didn't secure a single contract. It was too hard, I felt like I was working for the minister of the interior. And no lie, the work we did helped the police. In any case, it was the only time in my life when I was thrilled to be laid off.

My last job was as a substitute at Pizza Hut. Even today this phrase resonates in my head like a Machiavellian echo: "Thank you for choosing Pizza Hut, goodbye and we'll see you again soon."

Obviously I aspired to better, but a person has to live. People who get to fill their refrigerators by doing what they love are very lucky. If that were the case for me, I would give thanks to God more than five times a day, it would deserve at least that much.

Sometimes I write things down in a little spiral notebook I lifted from Leclerc down on the avenue. In it I tell something about my life, what makes me happy and what really messes with my head. I tell myself that if one day I go crazy like my father, at least my story will be partially written, my children will be able to read what I dreamed. I'm kind of like a cat, it's as if I've already lived several lives. I'm twenty-five years old and feel like I'm forty.

A Person Needs Two Hands to Clap

IT'S LATE NOW and I'm on my way home. They're sleeping like big babies, no doubt, I heard The Boss's snores all the way from the lobby. So now I'm stuck with a situation I don't much like: open the door without making any noise, something that's not so simple with the kind of key we have, keys with CARE-FREE marked on them. They're ENORMOUS, twelve inches long, eight wide, all for a weight of about thirty pounds, they look like the keys to the dungeon from the time of the Roman Empire. Sure I exaggerate but that's pretty much the idea. Next, I undress in the dark so I don't wake anyone and I slide under my cold comforter. There, if I fall asleep right away, it's good.

To tell the truth I just barely avoided an ambush. My dear and unpredictable friends, Linda and Nawel, suggested we see a movie tonight. I knew that boys would be in the picture but I didn't imagine that they had a plan B and that the plan B was a setup. You know, the friend of a friend of a girlfriend. The guy in question, a certain Hakim, was supposed to serve as my partner for the evening. On seeing the girls arrive early, I suspected they were getting ready for something, I noticed that there was the smell of fish in the air. Usually with this sort of thing I see them coming with my naked eye, I should have caught that they were arranging a *Love Boat* evening for me behind my back. As soon as I saw the individual in the hat get out of his car to join us, I got the whole thing and I tried to do an about-face because I don't like surprises too much. Then seeing that, on the surface, the young man had some selling points, I stayed. Unfortunately, as usual, the barrels for this vintage knock hollow.

I had the honor of choosing the film; to the great despair of the rest of the group I then chose a Belgian art film that lasted two hours (which turned out to be excellent anyway). During the whole screening I had the privilege of hearing the intensely stupid commentary of this scam artist Hakim, I was ready to choke him just to shut him up. I could see perfectly well that the film basically didn't interest anyone but me and two old folks (if you're good at mental math you'll note that there were only eight of us in the darkened room) but at least the others kept themselves busy. They were playing a game of "oral exploration," a pastime that simultaneously develops the senses of taste, touch, hearing, and eventually smell.

Bizarrely, on leaving the theater, everyone was really hungry, so we went to get something to eat, and this time, it's funny, but no one asked me to choose the place. Mouss, Nawel's boyfriend, a man of good taste, had the hype idea of taking us to a trendy restaurant near Montparnasse, decorated '70s-style: the Space Shuttle. Everything was perfect, but Hakim the Scammer's manners clashed so much with the classiness of the place . . . one word came to mind and that word is "wrong."

The highlight of the evening came as we placed our order. Of course, Hakim put himself in charge. He called to the waiter, a tall, skinny, distinguished blond who held himself straight up like you learn at hotel-restaurant management school.

"Hey! Hey there, chief! Come over here would you? Can you take our order please, cuz?"

You would have thought we were at the fish stand in the outdoor market. In another context I would have definitely laughed, but then, I wanted to hide. At that precise moment if someone had offered I would have said okay to a burka. I swallowed my meal like it was a day of mourning then I faked a surprise migraine so they'd drop me off at home. So then I drank some coffee with Auntie Mariatou and told her the unwinding of the whole crazy evening, and instead of sympathizing she clucked like a turkey during my whole tale. Then she concluded with one of those magic phrases that have the ability to unravel the most serious situations and defuse the most charged atmospheres.

"Man is a jackal but what woman can do without him? A person needs two hands to clap . . ."

Auntie's husband, Papa Demba, still looks at her with eyes filled with admiration and love, he's one adorable person, solid and gentle, the ideal spouse. Their story, the one he told me anyway, is mad extraordinary. Of all the young women in the village, she was the one he noticed. One morning, when he was passing by in a wagon, he saw her crossing a field. The view from that day never left him—I think he was making a subtle reference to her unforgettable backside—and then he swore to himself that she would be his beloved. He belonged to the blacksmith caste and she belonged to the noble caste so the union was impossible, but Papa Demba's strength and determination won out over everything else.

I love that Auntie tells me these coupling stories, they make you laugh so hard you piss yourself. She always says that it's the woman who makes the couple a success and the man will be its downfall. Maybe that's a little extreme but it's about right. She also says that love is like hair, you have to take care of it.

Since I was thirteen or fourteen, I have entrusted all my stories to her. She's a woman who gives very good advice. She always consoled me when I had heartaches, encouraged me to have confidence in myself, and pushed me to become more feminine, which was no small task because I was a true little tomboy. Auntie's horrified by my big sweatshirts, long shorts, and tracksuits, so when I have the misfortune of wearing a cap, we don't even speak of it, I exasperate her. She introduced me to women's magazines, high heels, and makeup. It's taking me a while to stick to it.

At sixteen or seventeen, when boys started to get interested in me because I finally resembled a young woman more than a thug, I thought they weren't sincere, that they were making fun of me. Auntie was reassuring, telling me: "You are very pretty and very intelligent, let the boys drool over you. Watch the other girls a little and you'll see how much you're worth. As they say, you have to watch a lot of empty plates go by before you can appreciate your dinner."

I must have been ten or eleven when I lost Mama and left Algeria with Foued in my arms. Over there, it was the complete reverse, I never saw men. I was glued to my mother's underskirts, and all the other women in the village too, who stuck together and were responsible for the education of the children. I could get fifteen different smacks for one single mistake. I lived among a crew of women who spent their lives hiding themselves from men. I worked whole days sorting through beads and ribbons for Mama, who was the village seamstress. I stayed shut up in the hut. Luckily there was school, where I could talk to the other kids, and the little garden in the back of the house. I passed my free time at the foot of our little orange tree and watched the street on the other side of the chain-link fence, inventing stories about the people passing by. For example, I thought it was loads of fun to try to recognize through their djellabas the fat women I had seen at the hammam the day before. Once I saw the one who had the misfortune of scrubbing my back with a bristly glove that ripped up my skin, so I took devilish pleasure in throwing some stones at her.

Settled in Ivry with The Boss, I was shocked by the immense liberty, the fresh air. He always left me alone to play outside and often took me to the OTB bar. I remember, while he filled out his trifecta tickets, he let me play some rounds of pinball. Afterward, if I won, I was entitled to one big cup of hot chocolate. If I lost, I was entitled to one anyway. This is why I'm still unbeatable today. I played ball with the boys in the neighborhood and, like them, I pulled the girls' hair and stole their jump ropes to whip them. I went nonstop, no layover from an exclusively feminine universe to a world of men.

At the beginning of adolescence, everything got complicated because I matured early.

I was truly ashamed of my chest, which I hid under gigantic sweatshirts ten times too big for me, all the more so because I was the only one in the class already fully equipped. The other girls, extremely flat in every way, envied me. If they had known that I was smashing the goods down so they would seem smaller . . .

My first true trauma went down the first time I bled. I was convinced that I didn't have long to live. I remember writing goodbye letters, thinking about terrible things, the kind of things you consider only at the twilight of your life, like confessing to Elie Allouche that I had a crush on him. Elie Chelou, we called him, Elie the Weird, all the girls at school thought he was a big loser, but me, I thought he was sweet. Sure that my bleeding was a symptom of my imminent death, I also made the big mistake of giving all my Boyz II Men tapes to Bouchra, a smart kid in class whom I extorted money from and bullied into doing my homework for me. I was lost with all of it.

Luckily Auntie Mariatou was there to guide me through these moments, she's done a lot for my brother and me, trying to do what she can to fill up the absence left by our mother.

I know that around fourteen or fifteen is the "critical period"—that's why I do my best to be behind Foued a hundred percent. I remember that once I was a real mess. I spent my time outside, stepping and scrapping like some street kid. When the neighbors told Papa, he laid into me, but it didn't do any good, I started back up the next week.

I was tough and I fought like a man. I didn't scratch, I didn't slap, but I got in my blows: with fists, feet, knees, and eventually my head.

In Algeria, I spent the beginning of my education in a little communal school where girls and boys weren't even allowed to sit next to one another. We had a profound respect for the school and always showed great deference toward our teacher. For example, in class, when he asked a question, the student being asked was required to stand up to answer. Also, if one of us was caught cheating or gossiping, she was immediately disciplined with a cruel metal ruler; the sound was so horrible we felt a collective pain.

My mother and my aunts often said that a teacher was like a second father and that it was right for him to discipline me; they added that they should even discipline me one more time to show they agreed with him. A second father, that could be strange. I already barely knew the first one. He was the man who lived in France to work, who sent us money so we could eat well and so we would have pretty dresses for the Aïd el-Kebir celebration. I saw him two weeks every year during his vacation. He didn't talk much but he gave me hundred-dinar bills all the time so I could buy myself pretty things. I often asked him what it was like to fly, how the planes could stay up there . . . He didn't give me any scientific explanations and always answered me saying something crazy, that I remember . . .

When I arrived in this cold, scornful land I was a little girl, enthusiastic and polite, and in less time than it would take to say so, I became a true parasite. I quickly let my good old habits slide, like standing up to speak to the teacher, for example. The first time that I did that here, the other students broke up laughing. I got all red and they called out in chorus: "Teacher's ass-kisser!"

I quickly understood that I had to take control of myself and that's just what I did. Ever since, I haven't made bad progress. Like they say, I've become a perfect model of integration.

Practically French. The only thing missing for my costume is a stupid piece of laminated sky-blue paper stamped with love and good taste, the famous French touch. This little thing would give me the right to do anything and would get me out of waking up at three o'clock in the morning every trimester in order to go to the line in front of the prefecture, in the cold, to obtain for the umpteenth time a renewal for my residency permit.

On the other hand, you can meet some interesting people in these long lines. The last time I talked to a guy from I don't know what country in the East. Tonislav was his name. He offered me some Diesel jeans that he was running some game out of selling for half the retail price. We spent some time in line together, and the more I looked at him the more I found him cute in his old Perfecto jacket. But fine, it would be stupid, if you're going to hook up with some guy he should at least have his papers. I've had enough of being a foreigner.

There are also two guys I see often, two Turks from Izmir, brothers. One day when everyone was waiting in a driving rain, one of these two was nice enough to lend me his umbrella—it really touched me that he would get wet for me. Ever since then whenever we run into each other we talk and they always invite me to come eat kebabs where they work. "Free. No problem. Greek, skewers." I'll go one of these days, I know where it's located, just across from the train station, the Bodrum Sun it's called, like three-quarters of the kebab joints in France . . .

I've had some cool encounters, but you can't say that there's rich ambiance in front of the prefecture every day. In general the cops deal with us like we're animals. The bitches, behind this fucking window that keeps them far from our realities, talk to us about our residencies, more often than not without even looking us in the eyes.

Last time, an old man, from Mali I think, missed his turn because he didn't recognize his name. The good woman called out Monsieur Wakeri, one time, two times, then three times before scrupulously going on to the next person. He'd been waiting there since dawn and his name was Monsieur Bakari, which is why he didn't get up. A woman told him in Bambara that they had definitely already called his name; she tried to negotiate his way to the window because he didn't speak much French himself, but it was too late. He had to come back the next morning.

I remember one day when I was full-out ready to collapse. I was extremely tired. I had finished working at the bar at one in the morning and the customers had been particularly shitty that night. I was on edge. At four o'clock, I was already in line in a pitiless cold and it wasn't until one in the afternoon that my number came up. So I had a really hard time bearing the disdain that this old hooker behind the glass threw at my face. Lucky for her I had lost the impulsiveness of my fourteen-year-old self, if not she would be dead, drowned in her own saliva. I just let loose like some poor bitch, for nothing because all she had to do was gesture for the uniforms to come and throw me outside.

When my temperature went back down I felt pretty stupid. I hadn't even sorted out the story with my papers in the end. Result? I went back the next morning, eyes to the sky, and lucky thing that I am, I landed on the same employee as the day before. Obviously she didn't remember me at all.

Ever since the February 2006 circular and its goal of 25,000 expulsions in a year, there's a gas-like odor around the lines in front of the prefecture. Going right along with the trouble-some echoes of wartime ambush is this crazy little story a woman told near the counters. Her cousin had received a summons from the prefecture. He was very happy because he'd been waiting for it for months. He thought he was finally going to get legalized but it was a trap. They took him to the retention center and now he's back in Bamako. He didn't even have the time to say goodbye to his loved ones or to pack his belongings. Ever since I heard her tell that story, when I'm sitting on one of those hard, uncomfortable chairs at the prefecture, I imagine men with little mustaches in the offices who only have to push a button for it to become an ejector seat and for me to find myself back in the village.

A Rainbow After Weeks of Rain

TODAY IS THE BOSS'S birthday. I made *kerentita* for the occasion, a recipe that comes from my grandmother Mimouna—she taught me when I was living in Algeria. This cake, with its chickpea-flour base, is a specialty from the west of the country. I still remember when, early in the morning, the traveling salesman took his tours of the block on his old bike, calling: "It's here, the *kerentita* has arrived!" Then all the cousins and me, wanting to buy something from him, would leave the hut running, barefoot, dressed in simple gandouras, and not giving a shit about anything. Our uncle Khaled would go crazy: "Get right back in here you wild girls! You want someone to see you? The men are going to look at you, for shame! Come back!"

That made us crack up but if you were a straggler you couldn't laugh too much because he would throw his legendary plastic sandal at you. I still haven't cracked his technique, but he never missed his target. It didn't matter where he was throwing it, the shoe would turn over and over and finish by landing exactly where he intended. In your back, usually. He was too talented, Uncle Khaled. After so many years of experience, he was Africa's champion of throwing plastic sandals.

"How old am I anyway?"

"Sixty-one, Papa."

"Oh no, no no, we can't celebrate that!"

"And why not?"

"It's a fool's party, a party for whities who clap for themselves because they're one step closer to the grave—"

"No, don't say that, it's a chance to have a party with the three of us all together."

I handed him his best outfit and his most attractive tie. I could see that he was happy, The Boss. Foued and I pulled out all the stops: cake, candles, and even the song. Meanwhile our witch of a neighbor banged on the ceiling with her broom. Did she think she was going to keep me from singing? If she keeps pissing us off, I'm going to go down and break her body in half. Anyway we don't give a shit about her and we sang even louder to rile her up, the bitch, and that made all three of us happy. I love these rainbow moments after weeks of rain.

After that, I went and shut myself up in my room to listen all-out to the Diam's CD that I jacked from Leclerc last week —that said, I have to stop stealing, I'm way too old. I'm in front of my mirror with my roll-on deodorant for a mic, and I sing like a crazy person. Oh, if anyone saw me! It doesn't take much to be happy. I'm happy, I know that it won't last very long but it's good while it's here. I'm like a lunatic, I sing louder and louder, I turn up the volume on my hi-fi and I jump with all my strength. The music takes me over and I'm dreaming I'm at a Diam concert: she invites me onstage for a duet, we rap together in front of a euphoric crowd, I'm loving it, I raise my arms, my throat's killing me, my heart's racing. She lets me be the star a little and gets the crowd chanting my name, so everyone shouts: "AHLÈME! AHLÈME!" When it's all over we go backstage, exhausted but wild with joy. Diam's is still keeping it together, her mascara hasn't run, she's not sweating. As for me, three staff guys bolt in my direction with towels and makeup-remover wipes. Later we trade impressions while sipping a glass of Tropicana in the skybox.

A run of knocks brings me back to reality. This nasty-ass neighbor—a bitch *and* public servant, it's too much—is thumping again. I made her angry with my tall tales of rap concerts, but I don't give a fuck. She can uncross her arms or even call the police, I'll invite them all to dance with me. We'll produce a remake: *Dancing with the Cops*.

Then the ringing of the phone brings me back to earth. It's this brat again who won't stop calling the house to talk to Foued. I always tell her he's sleeping, he's taking a shower, or that he went out even if he's in his room. She's getting on my nerves with all this calling. I don't like her voice and she doesn't bring out anything good in me. She sounds like a little twat who stuffs her bras and who treats her mother like a stupid bitch. I have no faith in her. Sometimes Foued asks me: "Who was on the phone?" And so I swallow my saliva and lie, telling him: "It was city hall" or "My friend Linda." You should always swallow your saliva before you lie, it works much better.

I can't explain why I do that. Maybe I shouldn't, but I can't seem to stop myself. With my little brother, I believe in always doing what's necessary. As far as girls go, there's no rush. For the moment, he has to think about school. He can have girlfriends in the summer when he's far from home, like at summer camp. That way I at least won't know anything about it. Until then, he'll be putting some more software on his hard drive. So for now, the little bitch can keep running her psych tests and screwing with my brother's peace and quiet.

Right now it's tight for him at school. Just last week I was called in by the guidance counselor and things didn't go very well. I don't know, there just wasn't a particular affinity between us. At first I wasn't going to take any advice from anyone. And then I hated how this poor woman in the over-ironed blouse approached the whole thing. She was full of good feelings and ready-made expressions that you find in books, like: "the work of the suburbs," "to change the world," or even "for the poor to thrive." She read me, not without a certain enjoyment, some disciplinary reports from teachers who had excluded Foued from their classes. "Insolent," "violent," "disrespectful" were the three adjectives used most often. I couldn't believe they were talking about my little brother, but on examining some of the reports, I recognized his stamp and had to confess that it was sort of funny.

Student Foued Galbi urinated in the wastepaper bin at the back of the classroom when my back was turned, a disgusting odor invaded my class. I will no longer tolerate this animalistic behavior.

M. Costa, math teacher

Foued G. is a loudmouth. He plays the clown and only thinks of how to amuse the gallery instead of doing his work. He waits for a moment of silence during work with the plan to modify his voice and pronounce vulgar and shameful things like "DICK" or "PENIS." Then the whole class breaks out in laughter and I have to play policeman to calm the ruckus.

Mme Fidel, Spanish teacher

Report from M. Denoyer, earth science teacher:
Foued Galbi threatens me in the middle of class. I quote: "I know where you live, bastard!," "I'm going to punch you in the mouth, bugger, go!"
What's more, yesterday, Wednesday the 16th, hidden in the hallway behind a deceptive post, he called out serious insults toward me, I quote: "Denoyer has an ass face," "Denoyer has a fat ass," "Denoyer, your wife is fat."

Before that, on an exam day, he put a piece of chewing
gum in the classroom door's lock. I couldn't open my
classroom and had to postpone the test. I demand the highest
sanction for the seriousness of the deeds and intentions
of this young person, that is to say at least a disciplinary
committee followed by complete expulsion.

I asked the counselor of this random education if kicking a kid of fifteen out of school because he said his teacher had a big butt wasn't kind of an extreme decision. She simply responded that in any case in a few months school would no longer be compulsory for him and that if he continued on this path his dismissal would be the final outcome.

I ended the meeting by telling her exactly what she hoped to hear: I was going to let him have it, that this would never happen again, and within a week, he'll even be an algebra genius. Promise, swear, spit. Pttthhht.

These teachers, I swear . . . I had the same sort of ball breakers who do the job because of the vacation, it's convenient for them, and it has their favorite time of day—the sacrosanct coffee break.

I finally got out of that creepy office with the walls covered in public-service posters and photos of domestic animals. After half an hour in there I had that woman's number. It's crazy that in the end she's all alone, watching the collapse of one after another illusion she's created for herself about her job. So she makes a big show and that's what is noticed. She tries to convince herself that she's really useful here. She believed it until a few days ago, just before they found Ambroise, the school goldfish she had nourished with love, dead in the back of that slut Madame Rozet, the gym teacher's, locker. With a little luck this poor counselor will be transferred to Sarthe and everything will work out for the best.

When You Love Someone,
You Stop Keeping Count

I SEE THE MEN in green who are getting dangerously close to me.

"You're completely screwed! We told you that you should have used one! You're really in deep shit now—"

"All right, I know, don't make it worse, I get it. I'm going to assume responsibility for my stupidity and that's that. It was a mistake, an accident, I wasn't thinking."

"But I hope that you realize that this is some crazy shit. You got into this so idiotically, you even have one on you. All you had to do was use it, that's all! And you don't even have the means to take care of your mistake. What are you going to do?"

"Yeah, okay, thank you, it's already done, stop giving me shit, it's not going to change anything. I'll get myself out of it, it's fine . . ."

The girls are right, I really messed up. It's fucked, too late to take back my slip-up, I'm going to pay the price for my carelessness.

"Transit pass."

I give him my ID card right out so he can give me the fine. It's not worth the trouble to argue, I can already see in his depressed bird face that all exits are blocked.

Linda and Nawel, model citizens, ass-kissers to the system, meekly offer their Navigo cards. They salvage their reputations with girl-next-door smiles that respect the law too.

I surrender and hold out the magnificent green passport that justifies my existence. His sickly bird eyes land on the exotic inscription: PEOPLE'S DEMOCRATIC REPUBLIC OF AL-GERIA. I see that this distresses him, his head spins around, he is distracted, he needs his drops right away.

"Don't you have a document written in French?"

"If you open it you'll see that it's bilingual, your language is inside."

"Don't get cheeky with me or this could go badly, let me remind you that your things are not in order."

All this because I didn't feel like putting their damn purple paper in their fucking machine.

So I shut up because here like everywhere else when you're out of line you keep your mouth shut. I had no desire to spend my afternoon at the station because the cops, well that's another story . . .

The RATP agents break off, happy to do their work as they must, leaving me with this little blue paper that condemns me to pay sixty-two euros. And so I'm obligated to inject this scandalous sum into our drug addict of a state that always needs more. The girls offer to help me pay. I refuse, that just isn't right, but at the same time I notice that they don't really insist either. Then they start telling me about their Valentine's Day evenings, their candlelit dinners, their gifts and other things that you don't normally discuss on a bus, particularly at this hour on a shopping day.

At first I listen to them and participate. Then when they start talking about love, I tune out. While the chicks are trading impressions of their pampered Valentines, I notice a young couple to my right. They're well dressed and smell like perfume. The guy has a little bit of gel in his hair and the girl, she has a little eyeliner under her eyes. They're in a state of osmosis, it's impossible to describe it. It hits me that they love each other, they stare into each other's eyes all the way to the back of their retinas, and seeing them like that, I'd bet they could do it for hours. They touch each other a little, discreetly, they smile at each other. Then he starts kissing her neck and the girl wriggles around like a chicken, it looks like it makes her feel good. The guy plunges into her gorgeous bosom with the air of an orphaned baboon. You would think you were watching an animal documentary.

I was in love once too, but not in public, not like that, at least I don't think so or maybe I don't remember it anymore. That already seems like so long ago . . .

Right now I see couples everywhere. They come out especially when it starts to get nice outside. They go to the parks, the cafés, the movie theaters, and they go on like everything's normal, these places crawling with people in love. Who act as if nothing exists outside of themselves.

In such a state, there's such a tiny part of your lucidity left that a person could do pretty much anything. From my perch and by my count, I'd say we lose at least half of our intellectual capacity, maybe even more.

It's true that if you are stupid in love then you are truly stupid in your grief for a love . . . You spend your time blubbering, you cry until you destroy every last inch of your Kleenex, and then you begin to lose weight, burning some incredible number of calories.

It's wild that sadness is an efficient diet, but it works ten times better than any of these miracle recipes for "How to Lose Weight Before Summer" that stuff all the magazines.

At times like this your people worry like crazy and never stop asking if things are going better—and not just how things are going, like before.

You multiply your consumption of coffee, cigarettes, alcohol, and eventually drugs . . . You take up listening to sad songs and watching weepy films. You need to talk often and find yourself with phone bills ten pages long. Most of all you think only about one thing. At work you're reprimanded almost to the point of being laid off, and it's strange but you'd almost like it to happen. At home, you break dishes, and often enough you unintentionally fuck up the nicest piece in the cupboard, a gift from the family. In front of the mirror you have trouble confronting the tear-puffed face that you've never seen so ugly. And when you're obligated to make some effort, it's all you can do to put a little lipstick on without brimming over completely. At a time like this, you're at the end of your rope, and you can only find the strength to say bluntly to your chatty neighbor who has been breaking your balls since forever, really, that you honestly don't give a shit about her stories of the sick uncle in Brittany or the heat cycles of her cat that are so spectacular even the vet can't do much.

You don't give one shit about this or the rest either.

And then, one merciful morning, you notice that there it is, the load is lighter, you feel better, you sleep through the night, you go out during the day and give yourself the courage to move on.

A little while later, you happen to run into the relevant party in the street. And on this day exactly, you happen to look straight-out awful, and I'm talking about the kind of ugliness that you suffer just once a year. And there you go, that's the day you run into him.

It always happens like that. Nothing like every other way you've imagined this moment, the movie of your meeting that you projected in your head hundreds of times and remade over and over to infinity, running back through without forgetting a single detail. No scenario can possibly resemble this catastrophic reality. You are dressed like a sack, you have dark circles that reach all the way to your cheeks and a haircut fit for an '80s TV series. There you have it, validated theory as true as "the other line always moves faster" or "whatever your neighbor ordered smells better." There it is, no other solution but to run, to avoid him at any cost while pleading with the heavens that he saw nothing.

Me, in order to avoid ever being in that situation, I had myself vaccinated. I swore to myself that in the future I wouldn't trust nice guys, the ones who hold the door open, pay the check, and listen to you when you talk; because all of this is inevitably hiding something. A guy like that, I dodge him like the plague, he'll always be the one who leaves you in the worst state, who crushes your heart and your Kleenex.

He says that he loves you, then shows you the photo of his wife surrounded by kids that he keeps in a special place in his wallet in the middle of all his credit cards.

He says that you're the woman in his life, then brutally leaves you because you're supposedly too good for him. You don't understand a thing until the day when you see him walking around the complex with his ex—well, you're the ex now.

He thinks you're beautiful, intelligent, sweet, and funny, and borrows money from you often—but when you love someone, you stop keeping count. Then one morning, like every other morning, you call him to tell him that you love him but, surprise, the cold, cynical voice of the lady phone operator answers. She lets you know that the number is no longer in service, you will never hear from or speak to him again.

Or then he comes to pick you up at the entrance of your building in his metallic-gray Ford Focus, opens the door for you, asks you if you had a good day, and compliments you on your outfit. You, you feel beautiful, you look at him lovingly and tell him that you're good when you're with him. When you get out of the car he adjusts his balls and burps. You find this repulsive but too bad, you like him too much—you kiffe him. Then he uses the remote car lock, passing it over his shoulder, beep beep. You think this is super–high class, he's glamorous and you like that, and long story short, you love him. He announces that he's taking you out to a restaurant—see, that doesn't happen often. Since you're a Sunday-afternoon made-for-TV-movie addict, you think that he's going to ask you to marry him. But in the middle of your diet salad, he explains that he's met someone else, that she's a really nice chick and that he's going to head off to Grenoble with her. He's packing his bags next week so would you be a sweet girl and bring him back the drill he loaned you and all his Barry White CDs? And while we're at it, can we split the check?

I've cried plenty for guys. I often regret it after the fact when I think about how they are all assholes—and I mean all of them—and that none of them is worth a single one of my tears. At the same time, I cry for just about anything. I'm even capable of crying in front of fool TV shows like where the child finds her mother or the unemployed guy finds a job, that stuff melts me.

The day Auntie Mariatou went into labor not only was I the only white girl in the clinic waiting room, but I was also the only person who cried. The others looked at me sideways, wondering if I was there for the same thing as them. It's like I'm making up for all those years when my eyes were stingy with the tears.

When Mama died I didn't cry. I think I didn't understand what was happening, simple as that.

It was the wedding day for Fat Djamila, a distant cousin who lived in a neighboring village. Mama was in charge of sewing all the outfits for her trousseau. I can still see myself squatted down nearby observing. I could spend hours watching her work, she fascinated me. With her thin, delicate fingers she embroidered the Algerian jacket with gold thread, following precisely and carefully the curves of the design, never going outside the lines, never having to start over. During some long months, she created the seven traditional outfits for a bride. This was no small task: it took plenty of fabric and beads, because the bride in question weighed more than two hundred pounds.

I remember those long afternoons when the village women would talk about nothing but the grand event. Zineb and Samira in particular, the cooks who were always making fun of Djamila, couldn't do anything but jaw on about it.

"You'll see, the day of the wedding, it's going to rain the whole day. You know what they say: if a girl opens her lunch box in the kitchen to snack before mealtime, hiding from her mother, it brings unhappiness and it rains on her wedding day. She had to have done that a bunch of times, you know, since she's fatter than the Belbachirs' cows."

"Yeah, it's true, I wonder if she's going to fit into the dresses that Sakina has killed herself to make . . ."

And then they cackled like chickens. I thought it was kind of nasty on their part and wondered how they could dare to make fun of Djamila so viciously and open their venomous mouths without a second thought when those mouths held only a few rotten teeth. Mama let loose on them and told them that they were just two smug, jealous, bitter old biddies and that God would punish them for saying things like that. In the middle of the yard she yelled: "One morning, you're going to wake up without your tongues, *inchallah*."

I wanted to go to that party so badly I would have done anything. I was only eleven and I begged Mama to take me. But she refused, with no chance for negotiation. I even proposed that I sort her ribbons and all the fabric scraps, clean the barn, milk the cow every morning, go to Aïcha the witch to get back some wool, but there was nothing I could do, I had to take care of my little brother who was still just an infant and also she wouldn't be able to sit with me because she would be too busy dressing the bride. The thing that worried her most, though, was the long trip to the village. "These days the roads aren't safe, the whole country is infested with fake roadblocks, and I don't want something to happen to you."

And nothing could happen to her? I could sense that the climate was tense. I remember that you couldn't listen to music too loudly, especially love songs, and that certain words weren't supposed to be spoken outside of your house. People were afraid all the time, the curtains were taken down from windows and replaced with wire mesh. Uncle Khaled didn't want anyone to step foot outside of our house, not even to buy our *kerentita* ingredients—from then on the traveling vendor no longer came by our house anyway.

The date of the wedding arrived and death struck savagely. It came as a crew, setting its heart on this little village in which, at least once for one evening, joy had reigned. It was a true massacre, no more *youyous*—no more cries of joy, only cries. They killed everyone, even the children, even some babies as small as Foued. And it was not the only village that was razed. So then no one would really celebrate marriages anymore, the people were traumatized by these images of mutilated bodies and blood-drenched baby bottles. I remember having this dream where the dresses that my dear little mama had constructed with so much care were splattered with blood. It was Mama who chose to call me Ahlème. My name means "dream" in Arabic. Mama's dream was to see me have my turn parading in the seven traditional bridal outfits one day. I've never set foot in Algeria again, I don't know whether it's out of fear or something else. I hope that I'll have the strength to return one day, to feel anew the earth of the *bled*, the warmth of the people, and to forget the scent of blood.

Luck Aside

THE BOSS IS TAKING a siesta, me, I'm dreaming of a better life, and students are protesting in the streets of Paris. The local precinct calls the apartment for someone to come get Foued. My little brother hanging with the blueboys, that gave me a shock. At his age if I'd had a simple RATP ticket The Boss would have had an epileptic fit and beaten me enough so that I wouldn't forget it; he taught us to respect authority. Well, he tried anyway.

It has always surprised me, this strange gratitude that The Boss and the other men his age have for their new country. They keep their heads down, pay their rent on time, keep their records clean, not five minutes of unemployment in forty years of work, and after that, they take off their hats, smile, and say: "*Merci, France!*"

I often wonder how The Boss, who considers his pride a vital organ, could lower his head all these years without losing it completely. I'm not about to wake him up to tell him that his only son is down at the five-o, it's not worth it, I let him rest. I watch him sleep and he looks old and tired to me. My poor Boss seems worn out, bled out from having waltzed with his partner the jackhammer without relief, played out from having led this tumultuous tango with "Franssa" for nearly forty years. He doesn't so much as hold a bitter taste in his mouth for all this, but just all this nonsense in his head . . .

Why does Foued have to hand me such a complicated mess? Recently he promised to calm down, to make a little effort at school; he knows perfectly well that he can't fuck around, I thought he understood but, as Auntie Mariatou says, "Just because the snake is still doesn't mean it's a branch."

And now because of this little pissant I'm going to have to set foot in uniform central and that gives me some serious rage.

At the station entrance I run into a familiar face that I had already seen once in an office full of strangers. It's Tonislav, the hot guy with the old leather jacket. Right as I'm heading straight for him, I see him, frowning. I grab his arm as we're passing and, anxious, he jumps.

"You scared me, pretty girl. How's it going?"

"Okay, thanks! And you, Tonislav, things are good?"

"Me, I'm always good. What are you doing here?"

"I have to go find my little brother, he must have been doing some bullshit."

"Ouch! Don't be too hard on him—"

"Yeah, yeah, we'll see soon enough . . . Anyway, I'm so happy to see you—what luck to run into you here!"

"Luck? I'll teach you one thing today: luck doesn't exist —it's for fools."

"Is that right—just for fools?"

"Yeah, but maybe you'd like it if we saw each other not by chance . . ."

He raises an eyebrow and looks at me without blinking. It gets me laughing—him too. His big blue eyes squint and two sweet little dimples write themselves into his cheeks while I see, for the first time, a gold tooth appear that draws attention to itself and mocks all the others. He got to me, this guy. I have to admit he's attractive. I give him my phone number and he slides it, all proud, in his beat-up leather pocket. He's right, I would like to see him again, all luck aside.

I speak to a chubby, perverted cop who looks at my chest like it's my eyes. He reminds me of that zouk singer Franky Vincent, with his thin mustache and his even more lewd attitude. He asks me to be patient and points to the right at a coffee machine, signaling that I'm definitely going to wait longer than five minutes. I could have really used a little shot of espresso but the machine is broken—that would have been too easy. I pace, I turn the other direction, my heels make an unpleasant noise when they hit the tiles. It echoes everywhere and drives me nuts. I end up sitting down. I think about Tonislav and get myself dreaming of love in the middle of a police station lobby.

A crowd of people parades past me. There's a woman who came to lodge a complaint against her boss. In a loud voice she says it was sexual harassment because he put his damn hands on her ass and said: "Bitch! Get me a coffee. Bitch! Make me a copy." It was then that I realized there's a real fucking lack of privacy in a police precinct. Even if you're just waiting for a piece of paper, you hear everyone's stories.

And then I see my brother's friends the brothers Villovitch, handcuffed with a band of smug jakes, and I get that this was a family affair. My brother was arrested for a stinky plan that, as far as I know, he was entirely capable of organizing it, because Foued's real problem is that he's no follower.

Franky shoots me little languorous looks from time to time. I've been waiting well over an hour. I decide to ask him again when it will be possible for me to collect my brother, and then, all cheeky, he confesses with no remorse that he had forgotten why I was there. So after he gives me directions I hurry toward a door and don't bother to guess whether his hungry eyes are following my ass. I'm trying to keep my cool at the max but God knows that it's not easy. There Foued sits, on a bench in a little office that's way too bright. Seeing me walk into the room, he doesn't dare meet my gaze, preferring to lower his eyes. He's ashamed and he should be. My brother is handcuffed to a radiator against the wall and it hurts me like these guys in blue can't even imagine. Starsky and Hutch take me out of the office to run over the story, a big mix-up among the kids at Insurrection, between Foued and his associates and some guys from Yuri Gagarin, the projects next door. According to the cops it was all part of some amateur scam. My little brother and his accomplices resold a bunch of DVDs for one of the guys next door, someone a little older, but they didn't give back the right amount because the other guy didn't want to pay them enough, or some bullshit like that, a dirty trick by some kids who don't understand anything about anything. Then Navarro the TV detective and his whole crew searched Foued's bomber jacket and found a tear-gas bomb, a shard of glass, and a big steak knife. I could have told them that my-self—I turned the whole kitchen upside down looking for that knife.

That said, the idiot squad is right, it could have turned out really badly. One of the kids is in the hospital; according to my brother he has a broken nose and his mouth is super swollen. You'd think he'd been injected with collagen or something.

The little shit in question, I don't let loose on him at all. It isn't that I don't want to—at this precise instant I would like to make a bow tie out of his body. But I can't bring myself to react. I'm too overwhelmed. I gave all of myself to this little Foufou, who used to watch cartoons and drink hot chocolate with me before school, so I don't even have the strength to bend him in half, the little jerk.

I hope that The Boss is still sleeping when we get back.

1st d8

I FIXED MYSELF up for my date. I spent two hours in the bathroom. I put on mascara to lengthen my lashes, a padded bra to round out my chest. I used a blow dryer to straighten my hair, a mask to hydrate my skin, and a prayer to ensure my salvation. I thought about wearing a skirt, but I don't know how to carry myself in those things. I would have to constantly think about keeping my legs crossed when I sat and adjusting my walk if it rides up too high. In the end I opted for jeans, otherwise there's too much to worry about.

Of course I don't forget the final touch and bombard myself with perfume. Objective for the day: remind him of his favorite childhood candy. I went all out, I'm even going to wear high heels. I have a knot in my stomach, I'm hurrying and so I bump into something and then I stop myself for a second and ask myself why I'm doing all this.

On the telephone he told me to meet him at five o'clock in a café on the place d'Italie and then he added that he would be there at 4:45. So I'm clocking in at 4:40.

The café's called Le Balto, like a lot of cafés. Maybe later this place will be "our" café. Maybe, in a few years, we'll remember this day, and we'll reminisce about it with great emotion. Yes, I'm getting carried away, so what? Don't I get to do it at least once?

I settle in and order an espresso. Next to me, a very fat woman with an enormous bun is counting out some two-centimes pieces on the table. "Eighty-eight, ninety, ninety-two, ninety-four, ninety-eight, one hundred two . . . uh . . . oh crap! Shit! Two, four, six, eight . . ." I burn my lips with the boiling coffee while the barman methodically wipes the glasses. He whistles a song I don't recognize and then he starts singing some Brel, and then, that's when things get complicated. I feel the fat woman with the bun getting annoyed and then, all of a sudden, she tosses up into the air all the change that she has been carefully arranging into little piles in front of her.

"Shit, Diego. Sing in silence, you're making me lose my concentration."

"It's my bar, isn't it? I'll sing if I want."

"You're bugging the shit out of me, I'm trying to count."

"You just have to stop drinking, Rita, and you'll see, you'll count more quickly!"

This fat, hysterical woman turns brusquely toward me.

"And you, young lady? Do you count quickly?"

Without leaving me time to come up with my response, she takes all the change by the handful and scatters it on my table. She puts it everywhere, a coin even falls into my cup. Rita plunges two of her fat, bulging fingers into my coffee to salvage part of her fortune. Then I carry out The Big Bun's orders. I conscientiously sort out the change and make the calculation: there is exactly four euros and thirty-eight centimes. Satisfied, the lady gathers the kitty into a plastic Monoprix bag, leaves eight centimes on the table, and throws me a "Keep that, beautiful, you deserve it."

Right then Tonislav pushes open the door. Like a scene from a movie, he enters Balto's in a beam of light, I see everything in slow motion and I even hear music in my head. All the elements are there to make his arrival sensational. He has disheveled hair, a three-day beard on his face, jeans covered in holes, and the battered Perfecto he'll never give up. If with all that I still manage to find him attractive then it's well worth the trouble of spending weeks in the bathroom. I feel a little awkward and superficial now . . .

After that everything goes very fast, he shoots me his romantic poet smile, comes over and kisses me like it's the most natural thing in the world, almost like it's something he does every day, a common thing like tying his laces or lighting up a smoke. You could say he's straight-out direct, this guy, he has me traumatized, in shock, on the spot. Then he installs himself near me on the banquette with an astonishing calm.

I stay wide-eyed for a minute before The Big Bun explodes into a fat laugh that makes me feel like an even bigger fool.

Suddenly it's all too much, I feel feverish. Then I see Tonislav's laughing and I start laughing too and the atmosphere relaxes.

When I tell the girls this story, they'll never believe me because, and I swear on my mother's grave it's true, in normal circumstances I would never let myself be kissed on a first date! And then, holy-son-of-a-baobab-pipe, a guy comes and pops me one on the mouth as if it's no big deal . . . No signing any papers first, no one sent me anything in the mail to warn me, and I was just not ready, not one bit.

So then we talk for hours and I soak up his words like a true beginner. He tells me all sorts of crazy stories and I believe them the way you believe in Santa Claus when you're four. He tells me about his life in Belgrade, when he organized savage dogfights to earn his living when he was a broke teenager, or later, how he taught violin lessons at a school for girls. They must have drooled all over him like little slugs. If I had a teacher that looked like Tonislav, I certainly wouldn't have stopped going to school at sixteen.

In fact he's a great musician, he's played the violin for years, and he learned all by himself, with his father's old instrument, according to what he told me. He stole scores from the national conservatory and managed to get along fine.

What has me completely stumped is that in front of this man I barely know I completely lose my shit, not one point of reference left, content to laugh stupidly at everything he says. What the . . . ? What's happening to me? This isn't me, this dumb bitch with all the makeup who clucks like a chicken in the yard.

The Boss's Honor

TODAY MY FATHER is no longer a man. Our world is collapsing.

The Boss wanted to trim his generous mustache, he miscalculated his stroke, his mind must have been somewhere else, and he messed it up. When I got home I found that imbecile Foued rolling around on the ground laughing his ass off. As for the poor Boss, he was in his bed lying on his back with a piece of his mustache in his hand. Above his lips there remained only a formless patch. He was too pitiful, stretched out like that, you could say he looked like an old cancer patient on his deathbed.

"What happened, Papa?"

"Someone gave me *el aïn*! Someone gave me the evil eye!"

"No, no one gave you the eye, you just shaved wrong, that's all."

"And the other one is over there laughing!"

From the living room we heard the little shit's high-pitched cackles.

"Foued! Shut up! Papa, come here and I'll shave it all, that way it will grow back like new."

"I am no longer a man! My son has more of a mustache than I do. I'm never going outside again and I'm not going to work anymore."

"It's no big deal, your mustache will grow back."

"I've lost my honor! All I had was honor! I carried the flag high! I was proud and looked toward the sky!"

And so he started singing the Algerian national anthem while staring at the ceiling. Then he signaled at me to come closer.

"Me, I prefer the egg on the plate when the white is well cooked and the yolk runs a little, so I can dip my bread into it. I always did that at Slimane's café at the Goutte-d'Or when I first arrived in Paris. There were eggs every day. At that time I had the most attractive mustache in the place, I was proud, you know . . . I want to go back and see Slimane. As soon as I can, I'll go visit him at his café, soon, *inchallah*. But I'll wait for my new mustache. If Slimane sees me like this he'll make fun of me. Slimane smokes at least two packs of Gitanes a day, so he'll light a Gitane and laugh at me, and say: 'Monsieur Moustafa Galbi, without his mustache, he might as well be dead!' Listen to that spoiled ass still laughing, mocking his father, he has no shame! Tell him to shut up or I'll slit his throat, I'll take my Opinel razor and give him the Kabyle smile."

The Boss is sad but, tomorrow, he certainly won't remember the sketch that he gave me about his mustache. And then he'll maybe tell me again about the first time he went to the movies in Paris.

He and his friends Lakhdar and Mohamed got a kick out of sneaking in, entering by the emergency exit in order not to pay for their seats. It was the thing to do back then, it seems. Anyway that's what The Boss said.

He spent all his free time there. He loved American movies, Westerns, Robert Mitchum . . . He would have liked to have been an actor too, or a musician, or something like that. In the '70s he played the guitar for his friends at Slimane's famous café at the Goutte-d'Or and called himself Sam. He had some success, the devil. From time to time, when the mood strikes him, he still sings to himself a little but all that is way in his past now . . .

The next day I woke up tired. I didn't sleep enough because I spent the whole night consoling Linda who had a talk with her boyfriend. This sort of Big Talk always ends in a mess or even a slaughter in certain cases. While they had been together five years and engaged for a couple months, the guy explained to her that he wasn't completely sure of his feelings, that he didn't feel ready to commit. What a dumb move on his part . . . I know Linda, she can be a true witch, and she will make him pay for this one over and over. Sometimes it's better to keep your doubts to yourself and pray that they're just temporary.

Linda has loved Issam since middle school and she sees herself with him for the rest of her life, imagines him the father of her children, has fantasies about his socks and boxers and that she'll wash them by hand with "delicate wash" fabric softener, and especially, up until now, she placed a blind confidence in him. Seems like a mistake to me.

"Fuck this shit! He's crazy, this guy, talking to me like that about commitment. What does he think? I'm a telephone operator? He must have thought he was going out with a phone company like SFR or Bouygues or something to talk to me about commitment like that!"

I think that she still doesn't fully realize it, she's too mad right now.

Linda works at Body Boom, a beauty salon that offers body treatments and hair removal. Since she was a little anxious today a couple of clients complained about her.

She told me that she made one bimbo cry this afternoon. The chick came in to have some hair removed and asked for a Brazilian bikini wax, and Linda, because her mind was somewhere else, she did the job all crooked. This had me rolling because according to Linda it was more like a Nike symbol than a Brazilian wax.

I think she needs to unwind and she's going to benefit from this little couple's hot flash to let herself go some. She even suggested that we take a ride out to the Tropical Club Saturday night. I like it when she talks like that because you can tell that it's going to be a good time. The Tropical Club is a real one-of-a-kind nightclub, there's nothing like it in the world, you have to see it to believe it. When the girls decide it's time to go there it's usually for a good laugh. There you have to forget about the chic, flirty end of the evening. A mass of losers in an exotic-provincial ambiance is a thing to experience at least once in your life. The deejay, Patrick-Romuald, a West Indian guy around thirty with an accent that fell straight out of a palm tree, has the art and the style to give the floor some atmosphere. He intros each piece and never forgets to rally the troops.

"Come on, gentlemen, get up and move your booty. Go find the ladies, now is the time to ask the *chabines* to dance! I'm the emcee tonight, the life of this extraordinary evening, so let me introduce myself: Patrick-Romuald, aka 'the Alligator with teeth sharpened for grabbing *chabine* bumps . . .' Oooh! A little joke from Pointe-à-Pitre, West Indies . . . Good night and I promise you some *frotti-frotta* tonight!"

When you ask Patrick-Romuald why the nights he runs the Tropical Club end at four A.M. instead of six A.M. like most other clubs, he answers with a malicious smile:

"Young ladies, you already know that the parties at the Tropical Club are nothing like 'most other clubs' and if Patrick-Romuald parties end specifically at four A.M. it's simply because anyone who hasn't found a piece to take home by four A.M. is a loser! And anyone who has found someone, after four A.M., well, he wants to do more than dance . . ."

•   •   •

Now all we have to do is convince Nawel to unglue herself from Mouss, her leech of a boyfriend, whom I actually like but who's a little sticky-clingy for my taste. Never one without the other, even worse than a couple — they're like a pair of socks.

Mouss, he's THE hot thing in the neighborhood, he's always provoked passions around Insurrection. When he walks by, the girls whip their claws out, rip their panties, break chairs over each other. One smile, one look from him and a crowd of women are at his feet, even more than for Claude François, more than Patrick Sabatier. You have to be brave to take on a guy like that and not be afraid of all the competition. Nawel was tough, she even fought with Sabrina Achour for this guy. And if you know Achour's record and animal physique you can consider Nawel's feat a proof of a great love. I hope she'll be on for the Tropical Club and that she won't play the little woman of the house this Saturday night.

The Gibbon

I SPENT THE AFTERNOON at Auntie Mariatou's house. She gave me braids flat on the top of my head, American style, with strands that cross each other. I ask for this hairstyle often, especially since I saw the clip of Alicia Keys on MTV, the one where she sings for the guy who's in jail while she's playing the piano with her eyes closed. While she's doing my hair we watch a program on TV about a couple torn apart by jealousy, Auntie's comments were so delicious I laughed until it made me tired. The man's name was Tony and his wife was Marjorie. Tony is tall, handsome, muscular, and he loves his mother very much. Marjorie is little, plump, stutters, riddled with complexes, and very, very jealous. She checks her man's cell-phone messages, calls him every five to eight minutes when he goes out with his boys, and when they walk in the street together she never stops watching him to make sure that he doesn't cruise other women, that is the ones who aren't little, plump, stutterers with complexes. If he ever had the misfortune of getting caught looking at a woman, there you'd have it, the drama of the century, a public scandal, a real bloodbath. Then, in the program, each of them tells the camera about their unhappiness, with the tears to prove it.

Auntie was one hundred percent into the program. So when we were watching she was really irritating me and pulling at my head like a savage. I thought she was going to end up scalping me. She spoke to Tony like he was right in front of her.

"But you're crazy for staying with a lunatic like that! She's really sick! Are you a man or not? You let her go, a handsome man like you, tomorrow you leave her, tomorrow you find another woman better than her . . . Ooooh, and then he goes back to her, that's serious . . . He's a victim, this guy, as they say, 'The lizard's tail is tough, the more you cut it the faster it grows.'"

So we were in the middle of an intense, refreshing cultural activity when, all of a sudden, Papa Demba shot into the apartment like an arrow. He charged toward the bookcase in the living room, pounced on the dictionary, and started turning the pages like a wild man. Auntie and me, all surprised, watched him out of the corner of our eyes. He ripped through the dictionary pages with a finger he wet with his tongue, his eyebrows knit together, as if his life depended on the definition he was seeking.

He quickly raised Auntie's sugar levels, irritated enough already, she couldn't stop herself from asking him what he was looking for in his frenetic quest.

"What has you springing on the dictionary like a rabbit on the run? What are you looking for?"

"I'm looking for the word 'gibbon'!" he said, carefully articulating this mysterious word.

"Gibbon?"

"Yes, exactly."

"*Starfoullah!* And why? Where did this fever come from?"

"Just now at the square near the Vitry city hall I was questioned by the police, they verified my papers, as usual, standard operating procedure and all . . . fine, and then, when they let me go, they were snickering to each other and said: 'Go on, gibbon!' I would just like to know what they were talking about because I don't know that word."

"And so, what does it mean?"

"Wait a second, I'm only in the *F*s."

He didn't want to read the definition all the way through. "Species of anthropoid monkey from Asia that has no tail, with a large black face, they climb trees with agility due to their extremely long arms . . ."

Papa Demba closed the French dictionary with a sigh that contained within it not a few other stories like this one.

Then he left the room. And Auntie Mariatou said: "Well there you go. All that fuss for that! For some nonsense like that you got your whole body in a sweat . . . Tell me what you gain from listening to this drivel?"

To which Papa Demba replied from the other side of the apartment: "I gained nothing just like I lost nothing, but I'm used to looking things up, that's all!"

Papa Demba, the gibbon in question, is a math teacher in a high school in Vitry-sur-Seine and he's pulled aside for questioning a little too often if you ask me. When the cops ask him where he's coming from, he responds that he's coming from the high school because he's a teacher. And so then comes the final play where they add: "For sports?"

Auntie Mariatou went to join Papa Demba. "Listen to me! Monsieur Demba N'Diaye, teacher, son of Diénaba N'Diaye and Yahia N'Diaye, you are the glory of the village Mbacké, it is not worthy of you to give importance to a word you learn from a red face in a blue cap! Don't listen to them, those *kou yinkaranto*!"

I love it when she gets up on her high horse. She said all this while holding her hand at her waist and rolling up her boubou with the other. She looked like a character on that comedy show *The Clowns of Abidjan* that Auntie loves to watch. Then she put on some music — Prince so she wouldn't have to change it — and finished doing my hair in some furious rhythm.

I'm at the Café des Histoires now, a little bit beyond Porte de Choisy. I stupidly came here because I liked the name. I set out with my little spiral notebook and installed myself at the back of the room on the banquette, like Linda and Nawel. I ordered an espresso from the nice waitress and borrowed a pen from her. I've never kept a journal because I always thought it was stupid and egocentric. I prefer inventing stories, at least they're fun to reread.

Actually, there are plenty of people who write. Even Linda writes when she's sick of everything. The day when she heard that her boyfriend had cheated on her, she wrote at least fifteen pages, it was called "The Travels of a Vicious Cuckold." She was touched by a real delirium that day, I was actually worried about her. Then she tore the pages to pieces and never spoke about it again. If I ever brought that up to her I think she would be ashamed.

The nice waitress, whose name is Josiane, brought me my espresso with the kind of smile that makes you want to come back even if the coffee is disgusting. Curious, she asked me what I was writing with such an air of concentration. So I invented a whole life for myself, I imagined I was someone important, to see what that would make me in the eyes of a person I didn't know. I just wanted to know what kind of feeling it would stir in others and I decided that Josiane would be my guinea pig for this idiotic exercise.

"Are you doing homework?"

"No, not at all."

"Ah. So what are you writing then?"

"I write stories that are published every week in a magazine."

"Really? Wow, that's cool . . . What sort of stories? Love stories? Stories about crimes of passion? Because I love reading, I know all the books of Pierre Bellemare practically by heart . . . And also every Wednesday I buy *Detective*, I don't know if you know it but it's full of sordid stories, assassinations, rapes, children shut up in closets. If you want to give them a peek there are the last ten issues over on the bar. My boss wants me to take them away because he says they give our customers bad ideas, but people ask for them, they like them so much. And like I say, the ones you find leaning at the bar here are often the ones who don't have much to say, and they give them something to talk about. Don't you think?"

"Yes, miss, you're certainly right about that—"

"Oh but you can call me Josiane! My name's Josiane Vittani and I've been working here for at least ten years. Everyone knows me around here."

"I'm Stephanie Jacquet, but I sign all my articles Jacqueline Stephanet, just to keep myself anonymous."

"Delighted, Stephanie," she said as she gave me her hand covered in rings.

"Pleased to meet you, Josiane!"

"So if it's not love stories or crime stories, what is it?"

"They're more like social stories, I'd say. Stories about people who struggle sometimes because society hasn't given them the choice, who try to pull themselves through and find a little bit of happiness."

"And people find that interesting?"

Good question, Josiane. I hope so, deep down, but all the same I should have told you that I wrote love stories, of obsession and betrayal. It's safe to assume that interests people. But the story I want to write looks something like this:

It would be 1960, on a beautiful, sunny afternoon. A MAN would come looking for a WOMAN. They would have a date.

While he would be in the middle of parking his Vespa below her house, she would be watching him from the bathroom window and saying quietly: "Oh, he's so handsome." She would powder the tip of her nose one last time before going down to join him. He would be thrilled to see her, she would have missed him enormously these past days and you'd notice a stain on his jeans. Then they would kiss fervently. Then they would both get on the Vespa and take to the road. A light breeze would caress their faces and they would tell each other about the grandeur of their love.

Arriving at the roundabout at the shopping center, ANOTHER MAN would suddenly intercept them. In his hard face you would know right away that he was the villain in the story. He would say something like: "Hey! You two! Stop!" Then the young WOMAN would get worried all of a sudden and say something like: "Oh shit! Fuck! It's my asshole brother!" At that point a terrible brawl would break out between the brother and the MAN, all hits would be allowed, dirty punches, sucker punches, Trafalgar punches—punches that will have unknown consequences for years to come . . .

The brother suddenly takes the MAN by the neck and
says: "Listen to me good, coward, this is the last time
I'm going to see you running around with my sister, you
understand?" And then he would turn to his poor sister:
"And you little slut! I don't want you going out ever again
with a guy like that—black, illegal, Muslim, orphaned,
unemployed, with a record! Otherwise I'll kill you, you little
whore." Then she would try to defend herself: "But I love
him!" And the brother, pigheaded, would reply: "I don't
give a shit!" So the two lovers would be separated by the
villain-brother, a militant member of the National Front, but
the lovesick and valiant MAN would swear to return to his
beautiful girl . . .

The moral of the story, it has to be truly sappy, is that this
sort of love has no color, no religion, no social security number . . . I'm deep in my own world and it's very nice. Josiane
offers me an espresso and invites me back whenever I want. I
think that the Café des Histoires will become my regular spot.
I'll come back with my little notebook, stolen from the Leclerc
store down the avenue, or with my friends, or with Tonislav if
he decides to call me again. I would never have believed that I
would fall for an illegal Yugo with a gold-capped tooth.

There's No Point in Running
if You're Chasing a Cheetah

"WHERE ARE YOU GOING now?"

"Out."

"Don't mess with me, I can see that you're going out, so stop trying to be slick. Answer my question, Foued, where are you going?"

"I'm going to the basement to play video games with everyone. I'll be back in half an hour . . ."

"Who's everyone?"

"Shit, you're annoying. Everyone is the same as always: Abdoullah, Bensaïd, Hassan, and the brothers Villo, Nikolas and Tomas. I don't understand why you have to play the big heavy, the boys don't report to anyone—"

"I already told you that I don't like it when you hang out with them, they make you hateful, it's a bad crew, they're idiots and you're getting worse than them—"

"Their mothers say the same things about me."

"Fine, go, get lost, and I hope that it's not to go watch your porn DVD, you band of dirty little thugs."

"Whatever, I don't need to go to the basement for that, I have a TV in my room—"

"Ahhh! Get out, move it! Go on, get out! Don't tell me the story of your life, you little pig. You think that you can spread your wings because you're sixteen? Don't forget that you pissed the bed until you were eight and eight is only half of sixteen! And don't forget either who cleaned your little piss-covered swizzle stick back then!"

Around then he galloped across the apartment hallway like a crazy person, stuck on his sneakers, letting his mocking laugh ring out. The shit pellet is getting his jollies at the idea that he could have made me sick of him and runs off carrying his soccer and combat games under his arms. All the same there's no risk that I'll get tired of my only brother whom I raised since he was just a baby. On the other hand, the more he grows, the more I want to slap him every morning, the *chétane*. And he plays it close to the wire because he's completely aware of his powers of seduction. It's true that Foued is a very attractive kid, he has nice skin that doesn't get shiny, black mischievous eyes, nice teeth, a reasonably toned body for his age, and his golden rule, summer and winter, hair shorn almost to a shave. And if I ask him why he doesn't let it grow out a little he says to me:

"If I let my hair grow, it'll look nasty. With my frizzy Arab hair, it would be like I had a carpet on my skull. It's for street cred."

When he turned sixteen I let him pierce his ear but he had to earn it. He wanted it, that's for sure. When he came back to it a little later he had improved his grades at school and sometimes even did the dishes for me.

"You want me to dry, Ahlème?"

"Ahlème who?"

"Ahlème the sister I love with all my heart."

"What else . . . ?"

"The most wonderful, the most intelligent, and the hottest chick in all of Insurrection."

"Good, that's enough, not bad but I think you went a little too far this round, you degraded yourself. You shoved your pride way down deep into your ass, I can see that you really want this piercing don't you?"

"Yeah, I want it and I'm going to have it, no matter what happens!"

"You must be pretty sure of yourself to say that—"

"I mean, if my dear sister says I can do it, of course."

"There, I like that better."

So I ended up agreeing. Against my will, of course, but I agreed. All the same he deserved to be rewarded for all his work. The day that he came home with a diamond in his ear, I took it hard, I admit. I had a hard time swallowing it. It bothers me that my little brother looks like all those R&B singers and, honestly, less masculine than me.

But then I didn't give in on everything. Foued wanted to go to Leclerc together and have me buy him a blond rinse—L'Oréal Excellence Crème. That one, my good man, is out of the question. I would rather he tattoo a scorpion on his abs like Joey Starr, that would be less traumatizing.

He does take care of himself, the little idiot. Mornings are hell, he has a whole ritual, he races to the bathroom. He spends hours in there. He wastes all his pocket money and his school money on clothes and creams. I tell him all the time that it's shameful for a boy his age. My brother's generation, it's the "G" generation, which in their lingo means a fine thing, a tight guy . . . And not only is Foued a real, clean G but he also only hangs with G's. Their slogan is: "G or nothing." And when they pass by girls, the *djoufs* as they call them, they make like peacocks and the girls go into raptures in front of them: "Aww, look at the boys, look at the tenda G's!" which does nothing but inflate their already abnormally overdeveloped narcissism.

My brother is so bigheaded that sometimes I could really thump him. His tango with the blond rinse, I found the whole thing a little too much. Under the influence of the pop-psych books Nawel lends me now and then, I even told him that if he didn't know who he was anymore he could ask himself some questions about what felt out of whack and we could talk about it. He answered me, laughing: "Don't worry, I'm not gay, is that what you think?"

Bleached hair has been the style for a few years. As summer nears you see all these blond heads rise up from nowhere, a wave of little chicks walking around the neighborhood. That can make a style "fresh-groovy-smooth-now," but it can also scare little children too. It cuts both ways. I'm afraid that Foued will wreak havoc later. He's my little brother, it was me who raised him, but I think that he will be a real bastard with the ladies. I can tell. The phone rings a lot more these days and I regularly hear the voices of the little honeys who want to speak to him.

Today, despite myself, I had to referee a ping-pong match, a real pro event, like the ones with the super-quick Chinese who play so fast that you have trouble following the ball. Two chicks called one after the other, it felt like the words passed each other, except that Foued wasn't there right then. I cracked fast enough when one of the two took the liberty of telling me her life story and I sent her packing. I was cold, it's true, but at the same time she had some serious nerve.

"Excuse me, it's Eva again, I already called just now for—"

"Yes, I remember that you already called, you're not teaching me anything there. What do you want now?"

"Uh . . . I wanted to know if Foued came back yet or not?"

"You called no less than ten minutes ago and I told you that he would be back in around half an hour, true or false?"

"Uh . . . true."

"So if you know how to count to thirty, he'll be back in

about twenty minutes, so please be a good girl and stop calling because it's really starting to bug me."

"You his sister?"

"Yes, exactly, his sister, not his secretary."

"Does a girl named Vanessa also call your house?"

"Am I asking you questions? We don't know each other, I'm not your friend, I am not even your age! Did I ask you the color of your underwear? There is no Vanessa who calls here and soon there won't be an Eva either."

"There's no reason to talk to me like that, I won't call anymore."

"Great news. Bye."

I had forgotten how painful it was to be sixteen. The second honey called a few minutes later. Her name was, in fact, Vanessa. It's a good name for a little breezy. I didn't even let her have the time to introduce herself before I hung up.

I'm taking advantage of Foued's absence to clean up his bedroom a little bit because he doesn't really appreciate my intrusions into his "sector," as he calls his room. Fatal error. Tell me about the mess in your room and I will tell you who you are. And so I can tell you that Foued is a little oblivious fuckhead. Just thinking that I would clean up the cracked drawer filled with useless things, I find packages of multicolored condoms. I see that the Monsieur denies himself nothing. Getting ready to sort through the clothes all jumbled in the closet, I take out three big trash bags filled with women's handbags—Lancaster, Vuitton, Lancel—and as I go past them . . . I find a shoe box under the bed with bundles of bills. Not two bills, not three, not ten, not twenty or more. Bundles.

I can't even believe it when I discover all this. I'm crushed. It's impossible that this is his. But yes, it has to be his.

The first idea that comes to me is to take it all, put it in the toilet, and pull our old friend the flusher. As for the bags, I would burn them in the empty lot behind the hill. But this sort of nonsense is vigilante justice, the kind you see in moralist American movies where honesty wins out over everything. Only here, it's real life, and in real life I don't really want my little brother to shoot himself. So I don't touch anything without knowing more.

I prepared something for The Boss to eat, read him the newspaper, listened to him talk about the endless domino games he played at Lakhdar when he lived on the rue des Martyrs. The Boss was very good, he won every round, every time he had the best combinations. The others envied him, especially Abdelhamid, who always tried to figure it out: "But Moustafa, how in the devil do you beat your opponent and win all the points? Maybe you have a special technique that you don't want to share with us? Or maybe you put a spell on the domino games at Lakhdar?" Nothing of the sort. The Boss's only technique was to trust in luck. Someday I would like to succeed in following this life philosophy, only, too bad for me, I don't believe in luck, or trust either. Today I don't believe in much. I believe in Allah who is my only guide and in public aid too, thanks to which I survive.

The Boss is finally sleeping. Everything is almost getting peaceful again.

Foued's been gone for nearly four hours, not "half an hour" like he promised before he went down to the basement. Though now I'm not at all sure that he really went down to the basement, I'm no longer certain of anything to tell the truth.

He came into the apartment, playing cool, whistling the tune from some ad for pickles that runs all the time lately. He doesn't know what's waiting for him, the poor thing, I'm going to fry him up like a sausage. Sitting on his bed in the shadows, I watch him come in.

"Ahlème! Ahlème! Where are you? Is The Boss sleeping?"

He moves into his room, feeling his way in the dark and pressing the light switch. He jumps, surprised to see me there.

"Fuck! I nearly shit myself! You scared me! What happened? Why are you kicking around here in the dark?"

I say nothing in reply, just look at him. I want to rise up and annihilate him.

"Answer! What are you on? It's like you're possessed! *Naâl chétane.*"

I stand up, grab him by the neck, flatten him against the wall, and then shake him wildly like I have a rag doll in front of me.

"You little shit! Where does it come from—all the crap I found in your room?"

"What are you talking about? Let go of me! You're sick!"

"I'm not letting go! And stop fucking around with me! You want me to choke you? You know exactly what I'm talking about, asshole. The paper in the shoe box, the handbags in the closet! And the jimmies in the drawer, what's all that?"

Caught off-guard, he violently pushes me away. I lose my balance and find myself back on his bed. I stand up again and throw myself at him even harder. The energy with which I catch him by the throat shocks even me. I squeeze his neck and start wailing with rage.

"I asked you where it came from! Answer me before I kill you! Answer me!"

"Stop! Please stop! You're hurting me—"

"And me? You think that I'm just all right? I kill myself for you, I did everything for you!"

"I can't breathe, let go—"

The Boss is awake. His voice drags me out of my mania.

"I can't sleep. Turn off the television!"

"Go to sleep, Papa! It's fine, don't worry, the TV's off."

I take Foued by the shoulders and push him so he's sitting on his bed. He touches his neck like he's trying to make sure it's still there, that his head is still really attached to his body. I must have gone at him pretty hard, he's all red and his eyes are popping out of his head.

"It's not worth getting all bent, I'm going to tell you. The money's not mine. It's the big dogs', I'm holding it for them, that's all . . . I swear to you it's not mine, I swear—"

"You're holding it for them?"

"Yeah, I'm holding it for them. They pass it to me to keep

for a few days and afterward they come pick it up and in exchange they slip me an ace, leave me fifty euros or something like that—"

"Are you joking? What about the bags?"

"That's one of the bigs who trusted us with a little deal, that's all."

I sit down near him—if I stay standing up much longer I'm going to die.

"What do you mean, 'deal'? And who are they, these bigs?"

"It means that they give us some stuff and we have to clear it out, so we sell it and there you go. Then at the end they give us some cash. It's like that."

"Like with the DVDs?"

"Yeah—"

"Yeah . . . That's all you say . . . Last time didn't teach you a lesson? I swear you're completely oblivious! Did you think about the cops? What would happen if you got picked up? They'd want to come and do a search of the house. What did you think, my friend? The big guys are bastards, they'll use you as a cover, you understand? You want The Boss to have a heart attack when the cops come here, is that it? And me too, while we're at it? Fuck . . . I want to kill you! What do you want?"

"It's nothing, it's fine. And the big dogs, you don't know them. Don't call them bastards, you're judging them when you don't even know them!"

"Who are they? What are their names?"

"You don't know them, let it go!"

"Names, I said! Spit them out!"

"Champs, Cockroach, Poison, the Vif, Lépreux, Magnum are the bigs you don't know . . . It's a family, that's the ghetto."

"They're your family, you dog? Say it to me again, you asshole!"

"Stop crying, please—"

"It's the only thing left for me to do, blubber like a fool, I'm going crazy . . . But think about it a little would you? Did it ever occur to you to use what God put in your head disguised as a brain? You thought that I would never notice anything?"

"Fuck, what about me? You don't think there are times when I want to cry too? Even if I act like there's nothing wrong, it's only because I don't want you to worry about me, that's all. Just because I eat and sleep doesn't mean everything's okay. That's the street, that's how it is. I'm not the only one, and me, I'm nothing compared to the others—"

"You're not the others! I don't give a shit about the others!"

"You think I'm not tired of watching you work like a dog? Always running to scratch up some money here or there. The clothes I wear, I lied to you, no one gave them to me, the TV in my room, I didn't really borrow it, and the game console isn't Jimmy's, it's mine. All of it is mine. I bought it with *my* money—"

"You're not ashamed?"

"No, I'm not ashamed! You have to figure out how to make it, everyone does it here. You don't see. You think that you know everything but you don't know anything! You're just a chick, anyway, so it's not the same."

"That has nothing to do with it!"

"It's got plenty to do with it! You don't understand, it's like the jungle! It's eat or be eaten, fuck or get fucked. The ones on top, the chiefs, those are the lions and us, down here, we're the hyenas, we only get the leftovers—"

"SHUT YOUR MOUTH! IT'S NOT TRUE! STOP! Was it those big dogs who put this bullshit in your head? And you swallow all their programming like a chump! Just because they fucked up their lives they have to fuck up other kids'. They want you to believe that it's already a lost cause, the bastards! We have to fight twice as hard as others, that's the truth! I know that, so stop thinking that you're going to teach me about life! Who do you take me for? I thought you wouldn't be like the others . . . And school? What's school for?"

"Stop it already, you know well enough that it's useless. Even you quit when you were sixteen, so don't try to teach me that lesson. The bigs, even the ones who went to school, they don't have jobs anyway."

"Do you want to end up in the *habs* or what? If you keep going and that's your goal, you're going to end up achieving it, you'll have your place in the joint, don't you worry. What do you think I'm doing all the time? Huh? I'm working my ass off, I'm making it work. Your way is too easy. You're weak. Your money is dirty. You're going to take back all this crap. You're going to give back the cash and tell the big dogs that you don't want to work like that. If you don't do it yourself,

97

I'll go find them and tell them. You hear me? You know me and you know that I'm capable of going to see them, I've got balls, right, but it'll ride better for you if you go yourself!"

"I can't do that, I can't—"

"You're going to do it! This isn't open for negotiation!"

"It's going to cause me some trouble!"

"You're going to have bigger trouble if you don't do it. And the jimmies? What the hell's wrong with you?"

"That's something else, and it's my life. If you had a guy I wouldn't say anything to you!"

"Let me point out I'm not the same age as you. You're still a dirty little brat, nothing but a little piece of shit! You want to knock up one of your little hoochies? Is that what you're after?"

"I'm careful."

"Yeah, right . . . With all the dirty bills you should have at least bought yourself a cell, so your little honeys would stop driving me crazy calling here."

"I already have one."

"Oh yeah, breaking news . . . That's the best yet. Great! You really take me for a complete nucker! I'm outta here, I can't look at you anymore. I'd better go to my room. I would never have believed it, I can't even stand the sight of my own brother anymore—"

"Stop acting like you're my mother! You're not my mother!"

"SHUT YOUR MOUTH! SHUT IT!"

Then I couldn't stop myself from giving him the pounding of his life, the final blow, the ultimate bolo. I slapped with all my soul, used the last of my strength. I nearly took his cap off, a little more and his head would have just flown right off.

I can't look him in the eyes anymore. I stand up and go into my room, beside myself. I lie on my bed without even bothering to put on my pajamas, hoping to fall asleep fast and for a really long time.

Then an IAM song jumps into my head, one I used to listen to on a loop maybe ten years ago:

Little brother left the playground, he's just learning to walk and wants the ogre's magic seven-league boots. Little brother wants to grow up fast, but he forgot that there's no point in running. Little brother . . .

Yeah, there's no point in running, "especially when you're trying to catch a cheetah . . . ," as my dear Auntie Mariatou would say.

Tales from Below

I WENT TO AUNTIE'S house, beaten. I felt like a worn-out rag used for mopping the floor. I told her the whole story, crying, I was in a truly sorry state. She made me a coffee with the percolator that Papa Demba gave her for her birthday — since the acquisition of this machine she makes coffees all day long. She told me to calm down, take a minute to breathe a little, because she said I looked like a Kenyan at the end of a marathon.

Everything I told Auntie about the fight seemed to dumbfound her, she could hardly believe it. At one point I even suggested sending Foued to the *bled* so he could chill, but clearly this was a ridiculous idea.

"It's no good, he doesn't know that country, he shouldn't

discover it for the first time as part of some punishment. Even you haven't set foot there for at least ten years, right?"

"Yeah . . . You're right. I don't know what to do anymore. At the beginning I told myself all his bullshit was normal. It's not all that serious, it's just the age. But now he's already chasing after money. I don't understand it at all."

"If he keeps it up and gets caught by the police, they're not going to do him any favors, he's grown up now. You heard about the double penalties?"

"I know, Auntie. It bugs me because he doesn't get it. He doesn't see what he's diving into. He loves the take-home too much."

"He got caught in a vicious circle, that's all, what can you do? You can't let go of him. Get behind him. Talk to him."

"He's not stupid. He's a good guy, my brother, but he wants to be big, he wants to be rich. Sure, I'll talk a pretty game, but I won't be able to do anything. The more he has, the more he wants."

"As we say in Africa, 'money calls for money.'"

"I hear you . . ."

"Money calls money but the rich call the police."

So she managed to break me down. Just then her daughter, Wandé, came into the living room carrying her little school notebook in her arms, which she'd wrapped carefully in craft paper.

"Ahlème, can you please help me with my French homework? I'm having trouble with the calculations—"

Auntie jumped right in, I wasn't in any kind of state . . .

"Go do your homework by yourself in your room, and figure it out! You think we don't have enough problems out here so you should bring us some more?"

The whole rest of the evening, Auntie Mariatou tried to dissuade me from going down to the bottom of the building to talk to the big dogs. I didn't see much point in standing around with my arms crossed waiting for it to rain, but at the same time she wasn't wrong, it wouldn't be a good thing to walk into.

All calmed down, I thank dear Auntie for always being there for me and I leave. I'm like a bag lady with my cheap flip-flops and my light robe, my pajamas torn at the thigh. I have a horrible headache. My eyes are red and swollen, I feel like I drank gallons of alcohol. I feel like a walking hangover.

Of course, instead of going back to my house, I went downstairs.

I went directly to block 30, the most high-risk spot in the neighborhood, the place where people are usually afraid to go out, the place where even the special anticrime brigade dreads going when they have to train someone.

I take a hesitant step into the poorly lit hall. There are three guys leaning their backs against the wall. I stand petrified for a few seconds in front of them, not knowing what to say to them or at least not knowing how to begin. The slight odor of shit is already starting to suffocate me and, mixed with the open Dumpsters, I'm afraid it's going to make me puke. The first gentleman, the one whose head is just below the inscription FUCK SARKO, speaks to me:

"What are you looking for? What are you doing here?"

"I'm looking for some people."

"What do you want?"

"It's for my little brother."

"Who's your little brother?"

"His name's Foued."

"Oh yeah, the little Orphan Arab?"

"His name is Foued."

"Who do you want to see?"

"Magnum, Lépreux, Cockroach, and I don't know who else . . ."

He's bizarre, this guy, he seems high and he looks me up and down in a funny way. I don't know what made me rush down here at this late hour, they're going to think that I came looking for something shady.

Then one of the guys at the pulls back his hood and comes toward me. The moment he gets into the nasty neon light, I recognize Didier, the ice cream maker's son, a boy I grew up with, I cheated at school with, who stole with me at the supermarket, who slipped me my first tongue kiss, even. I'm dumbstruck. He seems stunned too.

"No way! Back from the past! Ahlème, the Bomb! What the hell are you doing here?"

"And you, what the hell are you doing here? I haven't seen you for years and years."

"I was doing some time . . ."

What happened to me out there was a like a bad scene from a TV movie, but it went down exactly like that. So then he slipped me a kiss full of fraternity and good memories. It all got so sweet that I didn't know how to bring up the problem anymore.

"You know this *djouf*, Cockroach?"

"Yeah yeah, I know her, don't worry."

As if it wasn't obvious. And I hate it when people talk about me in the third person when I'm standing right there.

"So you're the one they call Cockroach?"

"Yeah."

He lowers his head, a little embarrassed.

"Crazy . . . and when people call you Cockroach you respond?"

"Well yeah . . . I don't know."

"Where does that nickname come from?"

He starts laughing and the other guys crack up too. One of them asks for some rolling papers from Didier. He gets them out of his pocket and gives them to the guy, a little ashamed in front of me.

"Cockroach, it's a trip you know, they've been calling me that for a long time . . . Because these bastards here, one day, they were giving me shit and there was a little cockroach that crawled out of my jacket, right. It's like that in the apartments around here . . . ever since they stopped sending the guys who do their thing with the spray, they're all over. And afterward, there you go, it just kept on from there . . . But that doesn't mean that I have bugs in my pockets, and I'm not dirty either, it's just a joke . . . They've got ghetto names too: he's Stray Dog and that one over there, that's Escobar."

"Escobar? After Pablo Escobar?"

"Yeah, that's right, like that . . . His real name's Alain, the great myth!" he says, laughing. "You know that fucker is a legend! Alain my brother!"

"Fuck you, asshole, you're nothing but a dirty dog, and your name is Didier!" answers the other guy straight off.

"Yeah but Alain is worse! And your mother's name is Bertha!"

"Shut your mouth, I didn't say anything about your mother, let it be—"

"He's right, it's worse! It's true!"

The other guy who was quiet up until then can't resist his turn.

"Don't even talk, Mouloud, Moulud the Grinder, with your grocery-store name."

"I'm going to fuck you up."

"No, I'm going to fuck you up—"

"Uh . . . excuse me, Didier, can I speak to you about something?"

We stepped outside so we could get away. I didn't have a jacket, I shivered a little.

"You don't have to be scared, what is it?"

"I'm not scared."

Tonight it's not Cockroach I'm talking to but Didier. In simple words I explain the situation that's got me angry and indignant. I tell him all my worries and fears, I tell him how my brother and me, we keep hopping from one foot to the other in this *bled*, because we have to be careful, we weren't born here. He must have heard talk about people getting expelled. What I was telling him was the real story, no legend. If Foued didn't keep quiet from now on the cops would be merciless with him. And my big speech, it wasn't just for my brother. I asked Didier and his boys to stop ruining the kids' lives like they ruined their own. I know that I'm not going to change the system, it's bizness and everything, but Foued's only sixteen. Shit.

Didier's not a bad guy. He's done some low-down shit, that's for sure, but the really bad guys don't hang out in the hall at number 30. The real villains, sitting in their comfortable armchairs, decide *who* is going to troll the halls at number 30. They're the ones who can decide to chuck a guy like Foued out of France for any little thing. Didier, he can understand that. He had wishes, dreams, those kinds of things . . . He probably doesn't even remember having told me, but he wanted to have a boat, one with white sails, ever since the time when his father gave us Italian ices behind the backs of all the other kids. Only Didier, he thought he could never sail a boat because in Ivry there's no ocean.

When we start to break it down, I notice that he is in all the schemes that my brother was mixed up with. He apologizes, swears on his mother's head that he's sorry, promises me that he didn't know that Foued was my brother. I wonder if he isn't just talking out of his ass, maybe it's just the spliff that he's smoking that's making him say all that. But I believe at heart, he's sincere.

"We'll keep him at a distance, your little brother, you're right. I guarantee it, and I'll be paying attention. Everyone around here knows who I am, and don't worry, they'll listen. Cockroach, he's not just anybody. And if you need me, I'll be there. I'll watch over him, I swear to you on the life of my race, I give you my word, Ahlème. No one will give him shit, no one will mix him up in the business. Sorry. I didn't know that you were the little Orphan's sister—"

"And stop calling him the little Orphan, he has a name."

"All right, that's out of bounds . . . Okay. Sorry."

I leave, dying of cold. We agreed that I'd come back tomorrow at the same time and bring Didier the money and all the shit that was lying around my house. I thank him warmly and I thank God too, I thank him for having to do business with Didier rather than the other shady rat who calls himself Escobar, because that guy, he was liable to ask me to give him a favor in return, something disgusting in exchange for letting Foued safely out of the business. I was ready to do anything for my brother, even the worst, so I'm happy not to have to face that.

The Breathless One

THE TELEPHONE RANG. I picked it up and right away I recognized Tonislav's voice. His simple "hello" seemed like a spell to me, or even better, a blessing. He asked to meet for a date at Châtelet–Les Halles at the foot of the fountain, at Carrée square. For the first time in my life, I understood what it could mean to "need someone." Why him in particular? I have no idea at all. I am completely turned upside down, my heart beats ten thousand times an hour just at the thought of seeing him. My knees wobble, I feel like I'm a clueless teenager going on her first date. I must be a pitiful thing to see.

On my way to meet him, sitting in my RER, I tell myself that I'll be bold when I see him.

I give myself the goal of greeting him with a kiss and asking him the favor of holding me hard in his arms, even at the risk of traumatizing him and having him not call me ever again. Today, without really understanding why, I just want to abandon myself to the sort of thing that I usually think is too sappy. I will let him discover all the weaknesses that I kill myself to hide from the whole world, and from myself most of all. And too bad if he freaks. That would just tell me that he's a jerk like all the others and he's not worth the trouble in the end. This time I'm not all tricked out. I'm just me and I don't give a shit about the rest.

At Carrée square I sit down on the steps near the fountain, I'm on time but I don't see him.

There's a crowd here. It feels funny to be here in the middle of all this activity that I can watch as if I'm not even there. I look at the people passing by, running, just hanging around. I have the strange feeling that they're all happy except me. You could say that they live, thrive, dangle their joy in front of me on their faces without a lick of shame. Of course I know it's wrong but at this exact moment I'm having trouble convincing myself. It's like all these people had piles of dreams that I was denied. There they are strolling around, taunting me. I know what they're trying to do, they want to make me crazy with rage. And, well, they succeeded.

At this moment I feel like I've lost a game of dice. You throw the dice on the rug dozens of times believing so strongly in each toss. You imagine yourself already stopped at the glorious number six, but it's no good, the score is always low. One, two, or three at the most, never more. You shake them well in the small of your hands, blow on them, close your eyes and whisper a prayer, always nothing. I think at the end of enough setbacks, you have the right to be discouraged.

I feel like a little kid being punished. I am in the corner of Carréc square and I'm hoping for just one thing: to see a stranger arrive and to huddle myself into his arms. I am in a complete fever, it's really some kind of crazy shit.

A group of Mexican musicians set up their equipment on the square. They started messing around with their foot pedals while finishing up their last little adjustments. They're laid out a few feet from me and they're mad funny with their gigantic sombreros. I thought listening to them would let me distract myself a little. I didn't have any trouble guessing what they would start playing. In general, it always starts with "Guantanamera." As soon as they let out those first notes, I recognize the tune and tell myself: won, that wasn't hard to figure out. A few happy people are gathered around and partially block my view, while I'm getting impatient waiting for a nasty character who is incredibly desirable . . .

The worst is that I can't get hold of him because he doesn't have a phone. Every time he called me it was from a telephone booth. It's too horrible to have no control. This guy doesn't even know it but he holds all the strings for my marionette. I have no mercy for latecomers usually, but him, I'll wait for him. More than once to give myself courage I tell myself: "Fine, go, I'm getting out of here, I'm no victim waiting thirty years for a guy I barely know, this pisses me off!" But for all that, I don't get up. I stay planted there like a sad rusty nail. And during this whole painful wait, I can't count how many guys, including boys who haven't even hit eighteen, came to hit on me, asked me for a light, told me I was charming, asked me if I had a minute to let them get to know me . . .

With a cynicism that comes from the depth of my guts, I tell them: "I don't have a light, I'm sexy on the outside but inside I have AIDS, you still interested?" and also "If you think you can get to know me in a minute, I must not seem all that interesting . . ."

And then there it is, I see a familiar silhouette from afar, wandering in the middle of the crowd. He's running. He was just a little late, after all, a good hour anyway . . . I start to seriously worry about myself in this whole scenario, not only did I stay here, alone, waiting nearly an hour in total turmoil, but on seeing him arrive I didn't even want to scream at him or make a scene. I only want him to wrap me up in his arms with all the passion in the world. Maybe I've seen too many TV movies but I don't care, I'm grabbing on to him and I've decided that I don't want to let go. He comes closer and in one jump I get up like a starving person you're holding a chunk of bread out for and I walk in his direction thinking of all the most beautiful wedding-march scenes in the movies. In truth, this guy could be a hustler with no kind of conscience, an assassin, a rapist, a slasher, or a guy who carves up his victims to steal their kidneys and sell them on the Internet . . . And me,

I continue walking toward him, a smile on my lips, my arms spread, and my heart in my hands. Then, just at this minute, I realize for the first time: "I'm in love with this stranger, he can make jelly out of me."

Before I even had to make the first move, he surrounds me in his reassuring arms and squeezes me hard, not too much, and not just enough, just hard, like I imagined. He smells like musk, his hair's flattened in the back, a single strand falls on his forehead and then there's his breath that I feel in his neck . . . all that sets my head spinning. You could say that he knows exactly what I've been waiting for from him.

The afternoon we spent together was surreal. If he hadn't needed to leave, I would have even spent the evening with him, maybe the night, or even my whole life. He read the lines in my hand, invented a life for me. In my opinion he doesn't know how to read palms, or even the lines in your feet. But I let him keep going anyway, it was nice, it tickled my palm.

And then just before we were about to part, he took off his old chain and put it around my neck. I kissed him with all of my one hundred percent sincerity to thank him for the gift. Afterward, he told me that I was a princess and that it was right for a princess to be treated like one.

It was very smooth but in my head all I could manage to think was: "You're very sweet, my man, but could you tell that to the slut from the employment agency, the woman at the family benefits counter, or even to the fat bitch who I had as a boss the other week at my last temp job at the Paris Bakery, I'm not sure that all these people share your opinion."

He left a little quickly for my taste, promising to call me the next day, which I believed without question, without even being tempted to shoot him my legendary "Yeah, yeah, right" like I always do with all the guys. I was on a cloud . . . My God, please let me stay there a little while.

Love Goes Around and Comes Around

SINCE SHE MADE UP with Issam, Linda has disappeared from circulation a little, she's now more scarce than a solar eclipse. According to Nawel, I get the idea that she is even more glued to her man than she ever was before. I talk to them both on the phone because they still think about getting all my news, but I get the feeling that they're drifting apart a little bit. We don't do as much together lately. The little cash I managed to get my hands on, I blew on physical-therapy appointments for The Boss, who's been complaining a lot about his back pain for a while. I told myself oh well, I'd rather let the girls enjoy themselves, take advantage of these beautiful days coming to them without my holding them back. And anyway it hurts me a little that they feel guilty every time they're with me, that they feel bad spending their money, telling themselves I'm jealous, even if they never stop offering me their help.

Foued and me, we're slowly getting back on speaking terms after our big fight. We're doing our best at pretending, but I can see that it's all for show, all *belâani,* as they say around here. A few syllables here and there, some jokes, asking to go buy some bread, to change the channel on the TV, or to take the trash downstairs. He doesn't hang out much outside anymore, I think it's been hard on him. His boys must be a little pissed at him, but they're not paying him much mind anymore because he was pushed out by big dogs. So he's home a lot, he doesn't even go play soccer at Coubertin.

This morning I received a letter from my aunt Hanan. Every time she writes, she never stops giving me a hard time, telling me to come back to Algeria with my brother and The Boss, and using her favorite technique: the guilt trip. In our family it's the fundamental basis for any education.

Your grandmother is old and sick. What are you waiting for? For her to die without seeing you again? We miss you enormously. Every time we reminisce about you here, it's the whole house that cries, with tears even pouring down the walls. Come see us, so we can get to spend some time with you and finally reunite our whole family. Our sister, whose soul is with God, left you orphaned, she surely didn't want us to be separated for so long. We wait for your return with great impatience, this great day, inchallah,

when we will celebrate before God and joyfully make our
reunion. My oldest children are all married, you haven't
been here for a single wedding, and they have sincerely
regretted your absence. According to my youngest children,
they have grown up not even remembering their own
cousins . . . So if God wishes, maybe this summer, fate
will reunite us again. Please, Ahlème, can you send us
a package with some medicine for your grandmother, the
blue bottles like last time, because you know that it's too
expensive here?

May God give you mercy, dear Ahlème, you will be
rewarded, inchallah, *your cousin Souriya wants to ask you to*
think about putting in two or three bras, Playtex Cross Your
Hearts in lace, please, may God keep you safe, you know
that she's going to be married soon. Sabrina and Raẓika, our
Kabyle neighbors, the ones who work at the Aïn Témouchent
hair salon, say hello, they would like you to look at the prices
for turbo blow dryers, they promise to pay you back as soon
as they can. Naïma, who celebrated her seventeenth birthday
last season, asks you for something she's calling "strings,"
I don't know what that means but she said that you would
surely know and then just to finish, I would like you to send
me the French cream for fighting aging that I asked for, I
think the brand is Diadermine. May God protect and guide
you, may he compensate you for all your kindness, and may
he send good luck to your house. Take good care of our little
brother and your poor father.

I wonder if this letter was really meant for me or if she should have had it expedited directly to Santa Claus. As usual, it looks more like a birthday list than anything. I feel like I didn't share anything big with them, just a few memories. All that seems pretty far away.

The day we left, I wore a little blue dress that Mama had sewn. I remember that I begged her for something that "turned."

It was Uncle Mohamed who drove us to the Oran airport. He turned us over to the hostesses, who were covered in makeup and who promised to take good care of us until we arrived in Paris. Then he squeezed me in his arms very hard. I think it was only at this moment that I really understood, while his beard tickled my neck and he whispered that I had to be brave. I realized that it would be really hard because before that day, Uncle Mohamed, out of modesty, had never allowed himself any display of affection toward me, except one kiss a year at Aïd el-Kebir.

I left my country, leaving behind me a whole part of my life. For the last time, I watched the Algerian sky from the window and I thought I would be going back soon. Since I arrived in France, I never took the road back to the *bled*, and if I decided to return, I don't know how but I would make a big comeback. But lately, I'm seriously considering it.

Nawel's maybe going to pull some strings so I can work in her uncle Abdou's shoe store on the boulevard de la Chapelle. He's about to fire his saleswoman because he found her in the stockroom with a customer. If the tip comes through, I could maybe finally get some long-term work and manage to save a little bit. With this I could take The Boss and Foued to Algeria, to our mother's village, near Sidi Bel Abbès, to our family home, Dar Mounia.

Right now I'm spending most of my time with The Boss because I'm not working. I savor these moments with him, I read his life in the lines of his hollow face, in his moist eyes, in his falling eyelids, in the curls of his hair that's gone all white, I tell myself that I would really miss him if he kicked it. When we spend this time together, exchanging pleasantries, he tells me his stories, and me, I sing him some songs. I listen to him with attention and I wait for him to take his siesta before I run off to the Café des Histoires to write down all his little tales. I've become a regular at this place, and it's rare that I get familiar with anything. When I arrive, Josiane already knows what I want to drink. She brings me my espresso and most of the time, if it's empty in the afternoon, she sits down at my table. She says that I listen well, that I inspire confidence quickly, and that it's a wonderful quality to be interested in others like I am.

The problem is that she continues to call me Stephanie Jacquet and bug me for copies of the papers where my stories are published. I can't bring myself to confess everything I've been brewing for so long.

Josiane never wanted to have a child, and when I asked her if she ever regretted it, she answered very precisely: "At forty-eight it's a little late to have regrets and then I know that I'm not stable, and it's better not to have kids if you're not giving them a real family. Anyway, you know that a pregnancy completely changes your body . . . I think that was part of it too, I didn't want to have flabby skin and hopeless breasts."

It's true that she's a pretty woman and that she's very stylish. Now and then she brings to mind old, bygone France, but I like that a lot. Josiane is on her fourth marriage and admits that she's thinking about divorce again, but she doesn't exactly know why she wants to do it. She says that she has never had a single valid reason for her previous divorces. I think she loses herself a little in all her stories. She wants to keep her first husband's name because she thinks that Josiane Vittani sounds like the name of a movie star from the '60s. She's funny and she's open. So like that, at the café, it's all good, but I tell myself that to live with her every day, that must really be something else.

"And anyway, at my age, it's not so easy, I'm getting senile, my poor girl! Just take the other day, he made the effort, the poor guy, to make a surprise and bring me breakfast in bed, and because I love surprises you would think I was very happy! Coffee, croissants, apple juice, the whole works! Oh! It was a beautiful spread, I'm telling you. The problem is that early in the morning, my head's all a jumble, like anyone. So when I wanted to thank him, I don't know why, I didn't know my memory played hide-and-seek with my mouth, but instead of saying 'Thanks, Arnaud!'—because my husband's name is Arnaud. Anyway, guess what I said to him: 'Thanks, Bertrand!'—except that Bertrand, oh God, he's my ex-husband. But I didn't tell you what happened after. Fortunately, I didn't make any other mistakes, I didn't add Frédéric and Gilles, the two before, the first ones. And the cherry on the top is that I didn't say I was sorry because I don't like to do that and it wasn't such a big deal anyway. Yes, that's right, I didn't even take the trouble to say that I acted poorly on that front. I never say 'I offer you all my apologies' because if I offer all of them, there won't be any left for afterward, for more important things . . ."

Then she plays out a sketch from the marriage service. She tells me about her husband's older son, who is, according to her, a sublime young man of twenty-five. She's certain that I'll like him and he would like me too. If I know what she's talking about, he's a subtle cross between Brad Pitt and Bill Clinton. Josiane says that she can introduce me to him. After all why not? I can give it a shot. I already wasted my time dozens of times letting the true social-work cases that Linda and Nawel insisted on bringing over to me try their luck, it would be hard for this to be any worse. And as far as Tonislav goes: no news.

After that, Josiane goes back to work, and me, I write in my little spiral notebook.

This is the story of a girl who grew up too fast and who was often sad. The littlest pleasant things were what saved her from her everyday worries, things that other people would think were boring, but her, they made her crazy with joy. She often dreamed of something else and she hoped that this something else would come soon.

One day, in the middle of a long waiting line, she met
a foreigner, a violinist whom she liked in fast-forward. This
poor girl, a little sheltered, grabbed on to him like the girl
on the Titanic *grabbed on to her plank of wood in the frozen*
water. She believed in him, in their story, something that had
never happened to her before, and she told herself that maybe
finally it was her turn to know the rapture of love.

Alas, just when she thought she was waiting for nirvana,
when she had allowed her heart to beat a little, that heart she
thought had been rusty for a long time, it happened that the
violinist disappeared without leaving a trace. She was so sad
that she discovered it didn't even do any good to be sad and
she promised herself to forget him forever.

I told Auntie this story, in its full length, in its full breadth,
and in *verlan*. She thought it was unbelievable, knowing me
so well, that I could have succumbed so quickly, so hard. Usually I nitpick for months and months before I crack, lots of
people put down their weapons before the end of the battle.
Anyone interested in me has to be extremely patient and motivated to win a little of my heart, a little of my trust, or to finally start a story together . . . And once it starts, in general it
never lasts for very long. Either the guy runs off before I can
even learn his number by heart and give him several ridiculous
nicknames, or I bolt first, because I got bored with him too
quickly. So now it looks like Tonislav broke the record. Euro-
pean Champion of Rapid Exits, in the heavyweight category
for mysterious disappearances . . .

Honestly, I have a real dazzling hatred in me. I don't usually need to cry at night before I go to bed because some clandestine tramp from the East didn't call me back. It's ridiculous . . . Nothing but bastards, all the same and, like Linda said the other day, "It's when you believe you've found the exception that you risk the biggest raid." In other words, it's when you least expect it that they give you the biggest fine.

Auntie Mariatou says that I have to let it be for a while, but I've been left hanging for two weeks already. For someone who was supposed to call me the next day, I think that's a little long . . . And she has an answer for everything, she makes an inventory of everything that could have happened to him, poor Tonislav, like he misplaced my number, had an accident, or fell ill . . . Maybe he had to go swimming or something, while she's at it. I've had enough of making excuses for everyone. And me, I don't give myself any. There's no reason.

I insulted him with all my soul, this crazy bastard, I used all the worst words that I knew, I even worked them into a few languages. I cursed him and his descendants, I prayed for the next seven generations to be born eunuchs, with four eyes and seventeen fingers.

Auntie says that I'm acting like I'm in a movie, that I'm not even thinking about what I say, because I'm not a bad girl and I'm only capable of giving people the benefit of the doubt.

Me, I say that he should never come back. And I am almost sure to run into him at the town hall one day or another. I didn't even notice in all this that my appointment date isn't here yet. I persuaded myself that if I see him, he will die of fear in front of me, and he will be ashamed, so ashamed that he will hide. And then, finally, I tell myself that it's all for nothing. The only thing I'm going to be able to do is to make myself more ridiculous in his eyes. If I do that, I will have given up my dignity for good, I will have condemned my pride to death. Negative. I'm forgetting him. Besides, I promise never to talk about him again, I won't even call up his memory anymore. I've decided to totally eject him from my mind, as if he never existed. Between Tonislav and me, there will be no regrets, a little like between the Danone factory and its two hundred laid-off employees.

The Life of a Stray Dog

I'M STARTING TO LIKE the fact that I have a real job.

I was hired for totally unjust reasons, nothing to do with my qualifications. I have this job only because I'm friends with Nawel, the boss's dear niece, and also because I speak fluent Arabic, and it's true that in this neighborhood, that can always be very useful. For once I can benefit from knowing people, and I'm not going to cry. Nawel's uncle Abdou is a very nice man, I like him a lot—at the store I call him Monsieur Kadri, because it's important not to get everything mixed up anyway.

From now on, my job is to sell shoes.

I spend my days among feet and I'm remembering that I really hate that. I think a foot is a truly disgusting thing. I'm seeing long ones, large ones, bizarre ones, dirty ones, old ones, fat ones, thin ones, and rarely some handsome ones. Some are actually infected. Sometimes I get the idea to take photos of the most horrible ones and make an album or create a list of the most unbelievable feet. Anyway I think I can even organize this whole idea into a commercial strategy: the winner of the contest for the ugliest foot will receive a free pair of shoes. All that just to say that I have some trouble with them, even my own, I even think they're horrible too. I can't bring myself to look at them. When I have to help a customer try on a shoe, sometimes I think about the Cinderella story and tell myself that if she had disgusting feet, with dirty nails and toes covered in blisters, the story wouldn't have turned out the same. The prince would have turned on his heels and run after throwing that dirty glass slipper at the bitch's face.

Now I spend my life in the middle of shoe boxes and unknown feet but I'm holding up. Uncle Abdou's store is really well placed, it's on the boulevard de la Chapelle, at the heart of the wild neighborhood of Barbès. I love this place. As soon as I have a break, I go walk around. I even make up little rituals for myself. Every day at noon, I eat at Monsieur Yassine's, the old Algerian who has a sandwich place a little farther up. His halal toasts are truly extraordinary.

Afterward, I walk by Kaïs's kiosk, a really special guy who seems like he's messed up somehow. It's very strange, this man never finishes his sentences but he makes them seem like they're naturally that way. I buy the newspaper from him and go drink a coffee in the tobacconist and bar across the street.

One day, on a whim, I went looking for Slimane's famous café at the Goutte-d'Or that The Boss talked about so much. I was convinced that I would recognize it right away if I passed it because it was at the heart of so many stories and he described it in such detail . . . I looked in the whole neighborhood, making the rounds many times in vain; finally I finished by asking two old Algerians sitting on a bench if they know whether this place or this Slimane even existed. One of them, wearing a checkered cap, told me that some years earlier the café had been bought and turned into a Chinese restaurant. As for the Slimane in question, the previous owner, he surrendered to cancer maybe a few months ago according to what the old man said, and his children decided to bury him back in the *bled* because that was always their father's wish. I stirred up something very delicate in their spirits because the two old guys started into a big nostalgic dialogue.

"Slimane, may God rest your soul, *miskine*. You see, my brother, those of us still waiting will finish the same. After having worked here all our lives like stray dogs, someone will send us there dead, between the four planks of wood in a coffin."

"Don't talk of unhappiness, God will provide and that's all, you know well enough that we don't decide anything."

"I know it, my brother. My only dream was to return to my home. Every year I said: next year. Then I said: when I retire. And then I put it off even more saying: when the kids are grown. Now they're grown, thank God, but they don't want to follow me there. They say they're French and their lives are here."

"What can you offer them in that country? There isn't even work for *châab* children and you think that *franssaouis* children are going to find any?"

"They haven't found any here either."

One of them turns to me.

"Tell me, my girl, why are you looking for Slimane? Are you family?"

"No, but my father knew him."

"Who's your father?"

"Moustafa Galbi."

"Moustafa Galbi . . . Galbi . . . Where's he from?"

"He's from Tlemcen, sir."

"Your father is Galbi the mustache?"

The two old guys break out laughing. The one wearing the checkered cap starts coughing like an asthmatic pig. He was laughing so hard that at one point I told myself: "We're going to end up losing him."

"I don't believe it, my friend. You remember him?"

"Who doesn't remember Sam! The old rascal, I never managed to beat him in a single game of dominoes!"

"You know, my girl, your father played in the café, I remember he played the guitar . . ."

"Yes, he told me about that."

"Oh, it's a strange omen that you passed by here. Tell your father that Najib and Abdelhamid the Oranais say hello."

"I'll tell him, *inchallah*."

"And tell the old loon he can come see us here, we sit here quite often."

It's possible that the old loon, as monsieur so affectionately called him, doesn't remember them at all, but I will tell him about our meeting anyway. I told them goodbye and ran off because if not, they would have talked to me for hours about a time I didn't know and had a hard time imagining. Since I'm too emotional, I think I would have been able to shed a little tear or two in front of them. And they would have thought I was the loony one.

I have to be a little crazy, deep down, because I always think I recognize that bastard Tonislav when I pass in front of the little Serbian bar on the other side of the street. My heart beats as loud as the Tlemcen *bendirs* and then, as I get closer, I realize it's not him. The worst part is that I'm disappointed.

The Right to Dream

WHAT I DREADED MOST has ended up happening and Foued has been permanently expelled from his high school. They didn't even really hesitate much. There was a hurried disciplinary council to which I was kindly invited and then the decision came down after some deliberation even if, it seems to me, it was made already in advance.

Here are the facts: during the year-end interview with his teachers and the guidance counselor, Foued explained that he would like to follow a sports-studies program with a section on soccer because it has been his passion forever—he has played on the Ivry team since the age of six. He loves it and what he would like is to become a professional. Here's the advice that the counselor thought appropriate to give him: "Don't go dreaming, it's unrealistic. I can't take the responsibility of sending you over there, not everyone can become Zidane. You should take a technical track in mechanics or electronics instead. I think that will suit you best."

Result: Foued, who was a little nervous, got worked right up. He stood up, started insulting them with every name in the book, most notably *catin*, which clicked particularly well with his French teacher—a real bastard if you ask me—who thought it was very ironic that he used a term for "slut" from fourteenth-century Old French when he wasn't capable of writing a sentence without spelling mistakes. He said this in a loud voice and it made some of his colleagues laugh. And there you go, no doubt it made him happy to put my little brother down at a moment when his future was at stake. Foued was expelled from the school system because they condemned his dream in advance.

I contacted Thomas, one of the special youth teachers who work around Insurrection, to see if he could help my brother find another high school. He explained that at this time of year that's no easy thing, especially given the weight of Foued's file. He said the best plan would be to repeat his grade and for us to look for a place for him starting next year. So that leaves us a little time. I asked Uncle Abdou to give me two weeks off. To convince him, I told him I was ready to never take another day of vacation in the next twenty years for these fifteen days now. He understood the importance that these two weeks had for me and gave me my vacation without any fight. I think now's the time. I reserved three tickets on Air Algerie.

I had to tell my brother that we were going. I think he was pretty surprised. He was in the middle of drying the dishes and he broke a glass from our Nutella service. It's sensible and practical, their being glasses. We also have a set that came from Maille mustard and another from Garnerth cocktail olives.

"But I don't really speak Arabic," Foued objected.

"Most of the people in the *bled* speak French, don't worry."

"Are we going to stay long?"

"No, not long. Two weeks or something like that."

"What are we going to do with The Boss?"

"He's coming with us. We can't just drop him down the garbage chute."

"He knows? You told him that we're going over there?"

"Yeah, I just told him. Ask him, you'll see, you'll get a laugh out of it."

We head into the living room to The Boss, who's in the middle of making little paper chicks out of the pages from the TV guide.

"Papa?"

"Here I am. Who wants me?"

"Where are we going, Papa? Do you know?"

"Gambetta, Les Andalouses, Bel Air . . . to Oran. Yes, I know where."

"We're going to the *bled*, right? We're going to the village too. I told you. Do you remember?"

"Yes. I've had it with the commercials on Channel One. Always commercials."

"Foued's going with us. We're taking a plane."

"Those crooks! Nine hundred thirty-four euros roundtrip. We're not rich. I can swim. It's not far."

Foued and me, we cut up at that. The Boss is unpredictable.

I have a date with Linda and Nawel. It's been forever since I saw their faces, I've missed them. We're meeting up at the Babylon Café near the mall in Ménilmontant where Nawel works. She knows the bar well because she goes there a lot with her co-workers. She says that it doesn't look like anything much but it's a tight spot.

I get there first, and from the outside I spot that it really doesn't seem all that special. I push open the door and take back what I was going to say, I liked the atmosphere right away: the lighting is soft, the colors are hot, and I hear a Manu Chao song playing. All the ingredients are here. So I'm a fan right off. Near the bar I see a strange character, a man around forty, with sort of a wild feeling about him, an extraordinary appearance, long legs, a sailor cap, and immense blue eyes, the kind of big eyes that tell stories. He sees me and shouts over: "Hello princess! Welcome! Sit down! What can I get you?" I ask him for an espresso.

"Why an espresso?"

The wild man has completely thrown me off. It's the first time anyone has ever asked me to justify my order in a bar.

"Uh . . . I don't know. It's what I always order, out of habit."

"Habit, that's what kills men. My name is Jack. But everyone calls me Jack the Weasel."

"Mine's Ahlème."

You'd think he's trying to make me crazy.

"Welcome. You know, I say 'welcome' because you're here for the first time."

"Yeah, sure. I'm going to order a tea instead for a change."

He shoots my order to the bartender like a tennis player serves a ball into play.

"A tea!"

Then the bartender, who has a smile Scotch-taped to his face, repeats it to himself like he wanted to remember it for the rest of his life. "A tea! A tea!"

I like that he's smiling. In general, when I go to cafés in Paris, I get the feeling that the waiters have a slot hidden somewhere in their bodies, where you have to slip a coin to get anything that could be like the hint of a grin. And there's nothing gross about that at all, is there?

The Weasel comes back toward me with the tea, which he puts on a paper coaster that's made to look like the globe.

"Thanks a lot, Jack."

"You've got some luck, you're going to drink your tea on top of the world."

"Yeah . . . I hadn't seen it like that."

"You must be waiting for someone you really like, it shows."

"I'm waiting for my friends."

"Ah! I was right! If you had a date with a court bailiff or an accountant, I would have known that too."

With these great lines, the Weasel abandons me as suddenly as he first started questioning me and leaves me to meditate quietly on top of the world. Shit, I spilled a little drop of tea on Africa, that's not cool, like they didn't have enough crap like that already. For someone who calls himself Jack, I think his accent sounds a little Algerian around the edges. But I would never ask him where he comes from, even if I became a regular at the café, because that's just something you don't ask. Me, for example, I don't like it when people ask me so I won't ask any questions, first of all because Jack works well for him and that's enough for me, and second of all . . . well, no, there isn't any second of all.

Linda and Nawel finally arrive at the Babylon Café. They're all tricked out, as always, they make a stunning entrance in a cloud of smoke from their cigarettes and their sophisticated perfume, the scent of springtime. They play the scene like girls who know the place, kiss cheeks, go behind the bar like they're at home, and smile to the right, smile to the left. I notice with great regret that Linda has dyed her pretty brown curls; she went all through with these kind of light, bleached, burned streaks and it looks absolutely messed up to me. What a waste. Worse: a crime against humanity. They come toward me in a pair. I think they missed me too, so we give each other big hugs and I invite them to sit on the banquette, like always.

"Didn't you notice something?"

"Your hair?"

"Yeah!" she says enthusiastically.

"You talking about this piss-blond dye-job? This stickup your hair surrendered to?"

"No! You're playing with me! You don't like it?"

"Not at all!"

"You see! I told you!" adds Nawel.

"But why? You don't think it's pretty?"

"Fuck, Linda, you're too much. You had the most beautiful hair in the world and you had to go color it with paint so it would look like all these little grungy super-skanks who go buy their panther-print thongs at the Clignancourt market every Saturday morning?"

"Oh shit! You're too cruel . . . I was aiming for a blond between golden and ash, it's going to be summer soon, that's why I did it."

"Man, you make me crazy! But what about the hairdresser, you had to see that she missed your color: it's not golden or ash, it's . . . smoky, like an old yellow."

"Fine, forget it. I am disgusting, I can see that it's ruined, but I wanted to convince myself that it was beautiful, but shit, I'm not a very good actress, so there . . . It's true, it's out of hand, I admit it. This stupid bitch of a stylist at Jean Louis David, she put these fat round disks in my brain, and I was so

135

bored, she managed to convince me that it was going well. And then I went and left her a five-euro tip! Come on, we're going back there and slap her shit, right? I'm hatin' her now . . ."

At that, Nawel the little thug breaks out laughing. Fortunately Linda is far from sensitive. With the girls, you can say anything. Since we aren't villains at this point, we suggest buying her a Movida rinse and giving it to her at home so she can be reborn as the beautiful, dark brunette who causes riots wherever she passes, the one men dream about in the middle of the day, the one who conjures up princesses of a thousand and one nights.

Maybe I'm exaggerating a little but it's just to emphasize the fact that she's much prettier as a brunette.

Probably just to give us a change of subject, Linda told us a piece of gossip all fresh, all hot, all wrapped up in golden paper. This one deserves to be relayed by the most successful American soap opera. They could do something with it, true.

A few days ago, Magalie, her boss at Body Boom, on the occasion of her husband's birthday, decided to go back to her house earlier than expected to surprise him. She asked Linda and the other aestheticians to hold down the fort without her and to close up for her just this once. Of course, like in all the stories that begin with "she decided to go home earlier than expected to surprise," the end is horrible, you can guess that already. So the poor Magalie goes home, she makes all the efforts in the world so that her surprise can be a success: she doesn't take the same way as usual, she's discreet, climbs the stairs without a sound, etc., etc. But of course all these precautions are useless since the husband in question isn't supposed to be there . . . You had to imagine too that when Linda told it, she set the whole scene in place, the tiniest details. Me, I prefer to pass over them because it doesn't take anything of the punch out of the punch line.

Magalie, confident and full of herself, enters the dining room to prepare this magnificent table that she had planned to set up so she could give her loving spouse a romantic, candle-lit dinner. But so much was her shock on discovering, on the couch that they had bought together at the giant Swedish furniture store, her pig of a husband in the arms of a young Asian boy of seventeen years! If I remember right, the end of the story, it's that she has an epileptic seizure, or maybe that she strangled the Chinese boy . . . or maybe that the Chinese boy strangled her instead . . . I don't remember anymore.

After that, Nawel, with no warning, took her turn strangling me. Without wanting to, she killed me. She always keeps really up to date on the news in the world, contrary to Linda who favors news that we'd call more local. On the phone Nawel told me about an article she read a few days ago that talked about a new expulsion of people without papers. She takes the newspaper out of her bag and starts reading out loud.

"You're going to see, it's some crazy shit. 'The man, twenty-seven years old, presented himself in the morning at the immigration office in the Val-de-Marne prefecture in answer to an ordinary summons. He came with no fear, in possession of a promise of employment that would allow him to obtain the much-coveted ten-year visa. Someone pointed him

137

to the room where he had to wait for someone in the administration but, to his stupefaction, there were two policemen who had come to pick him up. Headed for the local retention center. Then the first plane for Belgrade—'"

I rip the newspaper from Nawel's hands. The article is titled "When the Prefectures Set Ambushes."

"Quietly, calm down—"

"I need to see! I need to see!"

I immediately landed on the passage I was dreading.

". . . the minister of the interior denies 'having set traps for just anyone.' But the case of Tonislav Jogovic isn't unique. According to the organization Papers for All, his would be the thirteenth case of this kind since the February regulations."

The Other Side

THE FIRST STEP I take on Algerian soil is difficult, my body goes tense. I'm wearing a dress that spins and, since there is a little wind, I'm being careful to hold it. The sun in the *bled* shames my white legs that I never show.

The thing that comes back to me first is the odor, the scent of the earth, the hot air hitting your face. And always that letter missing on the sign: AÉRO ORT ORAN-ES-SENIA.

The mustachioed customs officer nervously rifles through our bags, he turns over — in every way — the bags I spent hours organizing, and shoots me a little shady look. No doubt it's the word *bakchich* I read in his eyes. Not a chance. I'd rather die in this airport than feed the beast of corruption. So he continues his performance, he settles our papers and continues to watch us in the hope that one of us will take a magnificent bill out of our pockets. Best-case scenario, one in the right currency — euros — and worst-case, a stack of two hundred dinars cash. He makes us wait with unconcealed pleasure, searching as if the eighteen passages to the customs booths and automatic doors since Paris-Orly weren't enough. Determined to achieve his objective, he calls one of his co-workers over for a "ferification." In reality, he makes a slight signal with his head and she understands right away. The good little woman comes over with a firm step, the mustache speaks into her ear — from what I see, they want to keep it on the DL. The woman has an enormous head that you'd think was screwed onto her bust. It's like she doesn't have a neck, she looks like the tortoise in the cartoon *Big Turtle* that used to run on Channel Five when we were little. She talks to me in a serious voice: she would like to know what the objects are that I have wrapped up in newspaper. I explain to Big Turtle that these are boxes of pills for my suffering grandmother. She wants to know more, so I tell her that she can open them if she wants. What does she think, this one? That I'm bringing ecstasy to my grandmother in the *bled*? She feels the boxes through the paper, rudely munching her gum, then I see her stop at a piece of paper. She gets jammed up there for several minutes. It's the best, this one, she's in the middle of reading, as if that's all anyone had to do. We're still waiting . . . But what the hell is she doing?

"What date is this? Is it today's horoscope?"

Then she returns to her post, looking dissatisfied. The predictions must not have been very good.

The Boss, knocked out by the heat, is even more out of it than usual. So he can make it through, I gave him a brochure on the security procedures that I stole from the plane. Foued seems straight-out lost. He looks everywhere, like a child loose in a shopping mall. The guy in uniform keeps insisting, then noticing that he can't manage to push us over the edge, he finishes by closing our bags and marking them with little white chalk crosses, which signifies that everything is okay. He grudgingly lets us leave, a little like a fisher would let a big salmon go. We take our bags and steer ourselves toward the exit. I catch him giving us one last dirty look, all the while twisting his mustache between his thumb and his index finger. I wonder what he's saying to himself, maybe: "These immigrants, what a bunch of cheapskates! With all that money they make in France . . ."

In front of the arrivals gate, people wait under the palm trees. The sun bangs against the windshields and bald skulls of the taxi drivers, who intercept travelers from every direction. They shout their destinations, the little villages they're going to pass through. Then the people climb up into the vehicle, throw their suitcases in the trunk themselves, and vroom, it makes a big American getaway.

We're waiting for our cousin Youssef. I'm not sure I'll recognize him, but he will recognize us for sure.

For the past few minutes, Foued is ready to follow every taxi driver who comes toward us calling The Boss *"aâmi,"* thinking he's the cousin we're waiting for. I explain to him that it's just a polite expression and that here all the guys who call each other *khoyya* aren't necessarily brothers. It's a little like the boys in the city and the way they call each other cousin.

Youssef finally arrives. The reunion is emotional but a little strange because, actually, none of us remember anything about the other at all. Anyway, it's no big thing. He's a man now, his worries have made him age earlier than expected, and except for the bit of an evil glint in his eye, the mischievous little kid I learned forbidden games with has disappeared. We get into the taxi and our cousin tries to make conversation with The Boss. He's having trouble but he keeps trying. I warned him, I explained everything to him so he wouldn't be too stunned at the difference. Besides, I warned them all that Papa was sick. They're used to it because of Uncle Kader, he's been like this too since he came back from the army—I wonder what they did to him over there. According to Aunt Hanan's letters, it must have been tough. He really bugged out. Apparently he pissed himself in the middle of the market and decided to get undressed in the street and started dancing around. Youssef asks us some questions, asks what we do, shows an interest in our lives. I tell him I'm working, but he seems disappointed when I explain exactly what I do for a job. As for Foued, he lies and says that he's going to school and that he works hard. He swallowed his saliva before lying: I can see we have the same technique. He avoided my eye while he was doing it. Maybe he was afraid that I would expose him, that I would shame him in front of a *blédard*, as he calls them.

"You still play *boléta*, Foued, like your sister wrote to me in her letter?"

"Yeah, that's right."

"Why don't you ever write us a letter?"

"Because I'm not so great at French."

"What about mine? It's worse than yours, but I write all the same. You're putting me on, little *Franssaoui* . . ."

That makes one point for the *blédard*, I'd say.

It's too hot around here, drops of sweat run down my forehead. The air is dry and the dust comes in through the lowered window and gets into the corners of my eyes. The taxi driver drives like a crazy freak and I'm going to spend two weeks with these people that I haven't seen in more than ten years and I don't know all that well.

The day before we left for Algeria I went to say goodbye to Auntie Mariatou. I told her some of my worries about the trip. I was really afraid of having nothing in common with my relatives, I was afraid that France has stamped me to the point of making me feel even more of a foreigner over there. So she gave me one of her succulent sayings, which I brought in my suitcases: "A wood plank can stay a hundred years in the river, but it will never be a cayman."

Just like I imagined, the entire village is on watch, a crowd is posted in front of the house. I don't know all these people expecting me, all these faces waiting for me, I wonder what I'll have to say to them. I feel lost like a fledgling bird who doesn't know where his nest is anymore.

The taxi parks in a cloud of dust and, on seeing the family house, Dar Mounia, something grips my heart. I'm short of breath, everything is moving too quickly for me. This is where I grew up, and the first sensation I have is that everything is small. My memory is right in front of me, only in a reduced version. We get out of the car and, while Foued and cousin Youssef take the suitcases out of the trunk, The Boss decides to make a real entrance. I don't know what came over him but he burst out of the car and set himself crying with joy, raising his arms, clapping and whistling. The craziest part is that the people picked up his vibe, it was like the audience at the beginning of an NTM concert in their glory days.

"Long live Algeria! The people of Algeria are free! We won! Algeria is ours! *Istiqlal! Istiqlal!*"

People are laughing, the children surround us. They cling to us, to our clothes and our arms. It's craziness. They start shouting:

"The immigrants! The immigrants! Where is Jacques Chirac?"

Then I recognize some familiar faces coming toward us. Aunts, uncles, and cousins throw themselves on us, hug us, embrace us with all their hearts. We are welcomed in a mad crazy euphoria, their shouts and *youyous* take us up, the village is in full celebration because a piece of France is paying them a visit. Then the ceremonial greetings, the "*salaam*" and the "*labès*," begin. I feel like a week has passed between our arrival and the moment when we finally enter the house.

As time goes along more details come back to me. I rediscovered my little secret corner. For me, all of Algeria could be found here. The fence through which I watched the passersby and invented stories for them had been replaced with a low stone wall. My beautiful orange tree has disappeared. Someone cut it down, replacing it with a water spigot and some huge ceramic sinks for doing laundry. Except for these things, Dar Mounia hasn't really changed.

My grandmother's grown old, she is sick. Having lost all her teeth, she can only eat soup and vegetable purée now. She spends her time sleeping because she gets tired too quickly. The poor woman is sweet for Foued. She has a particular affection for him because she was the one who rocked him as a baby, murmuring the traditional songs, and she was the one who chose his name too. The problem is that the little shit dodges her, because I think she frightens him: "She freaks me out with all the drawings on her face, and her mouth stinks too! She's like the killer in *Saw!*" He's talking about the tribal tattoos she wears on her forehead and chin. No one does them anymore, but in the old days it was a horrible test, it seems. In the village, there are some elders who used to be in charge of it, with heated needles, and apparently these elders weren't very fun, more like real hyenas. You could always try to escape, fight them off, but no way, they held your face good and tight. Grandmother told me that when they wanted to do it to Mama while she was still a little girl, she ran into the forest to hide. She laughed when she told the story, opening her empty mouth wide.

My memory of Aunt Hanan was true enough. She's melo-drama personified, she cries all the time, for anything and everything. When I see her eyebrows start to wriggle and her lips start to twist from top to bottom, I think: "Oh shit! There she goes, she's doing it again for us!" Fortunately she's never seen *Titanic*.

She talks to me a lot about the time when I lived there. She makes me look at old Polaroids, she even shows me the spot where I slept . . . It's like she wanted to bring me all the little things I would have lost along the way. She tells me that France tore me from the arms of my country like a baby is ripped from its mother. There you have it, she says something and so it starts, the wiggling eyebrows and the trembling lips . . . She has quite a few other magic formulas like this. Aunt Hanan, she could make a truck driver cry.

I spend my days listening to people, trying to remember who I come from. I have a hard time admitting it, but the truth is that my place is no longer here.

My young cousins have one word on their lips: marriage. They prepare their trousseaus, and at Foued's age they're al-ready real women. Their lives are stitched into their straw rugs as surely as mine is engraved into the concrete of Ivry's build-ings. In the afternoon, they let themselves fantasize about an-other life, far away and impossible, when they watch the Mex-ican soap opera, drenched in orange-blossom water, clumsily dubbed into Arabic—minus the slightly hot scenes, censored, because they can dream, but not too much all the same. This nonsense happens every day at one o'clock. So in the village at one o'clock, life stops. And after the viewing, it's time for the siesta.

It's exactly at this hour that poor Foued cracked.

"Shit it's dead here, I want to go outside—"

"But there's no one out there."

"What's with this *bled* where everyone sleeps?"

"It's too hot outside at this hour. You think you're in France, or what? If you go out now, you're going to fall down dry, you'll see. The sun is going to scald your skull."

The "cousins," the ones who live in France and are in the *bled* for vacations, talk about nothing but their new country. They talk about it like a close friend who sometimes reaches out to them, sometimes kicks them away. They relay the stories they hear, the accounts of those who have slipped through the mesh in the net, and they add some, never admitting their failures or their misery. They never tell their family in the *bled* that they work at night, that they wash dishes at nasty Chinese restaurants, and that they sleep in miserable little maids' rooms. They embellish everything because they're ashamed, but they still prefer all that over coming back forever.

Cousin Youssef, he'll never know France. He told me that half the population is at least twenty-five and, destitute, doesn't know what to do about its dreams.

I would like to tell them that over there, in France, it's not what they think, that through the distorting window that is the television, they know nothing real. The French channels they pirate to watch the TF1 summer shows don't show them the truth. As the young people here say, the satellite dishes hooked on the buildings of Oran are the ears of the city, stretched toward the north, ready to hear it all. But these ears are clogged.

But I don't let myself tell them all that, I don't want to be taken for Madame Know-It-All. These people have known a civil war, hunger, and fear, and even if France isn't what they believe, it's not so bad there, because here it's maybe actually worse.

After the traditional diarrhea of the first days, Foued has managed to strike up a friendship with some of the little neighbors. The kids around here have already nicknamed him "the Migrant." Together they spend their days in the area, hanging out in front of the *hanout*. His new hellmates, they're *bled* kids, real resourceful guys, guys who sell plastic bags, peanuts, or cigarettes by the piece in the street, who are going to spend their days digging through the trash in search of an eventual miracle or a pair of shoes. Even if we don't stay here long, I hope that Foued will see that money, it's not so easy to get, that these kids who march their dirty, aching feet in counterfeit "Mike" shoes, and who are beaten by adults all day long, including by their parents in the evening when they haven't earned enough dinars, these kids, they suffer but they get by and don't often complain. I hope seeing life here is going to make him think.

Today we're going to the city, to the ocean, and then to the cemetery where Mama's buried, while the brothers Djamel and Aïssa drive The Boss to the marabout's house in the neighboring village to do what they call a *ziara*, a sort of disenchantment.

The ritual is the same for curing insanity, for setting a curse, or for treating troubled children. We'll see what good it can do, anyway it can't make it any worse.

While everyone is getting ready, I plant myself under the olive tree in front of the house. I listen to Algeria, I smell its odor, and I write in my little spiral notebook to describe it all.

I even talk about the small wooden comb my aunts use to smooth out my hair. I talk about Isis, the brand that has the monopoly on laundry detergent here, and also shampoo, soap, dish soap, toothpaste, sanitary napkins . . .

I tell the story of the big party the first night that was organized in our honor, the sheep they fattened and then roasted on a spit, all these new heads I have to memorize in such a small amount of time.

I talk about my cousin Khadra who sticks to me all day and who never stops complimenting me on the Agnès B. cardigan I wear. She touches it, saying she would love to have one like it, that she looked all over the Oran boutiques, that she thinks it's soft, new . . . She certainly hopes that I take it off and leave it with her, but it was a present from Linda and Nawel for my birthday. Cousin Khadra practices psychological pressure on me. Foued was the first to notice her little game and he hasn't stopped himself from warning me.

"That's some bullshit, I've never seen the like, it's a sweater yo, you'd think she'd never seen a sweater."

"It's not just a sweater. It's my Agnès B. sweater."

"Oh yeah . . . So then the cuz, she knows that she can smell it."

In my notebook I don't forget to write down what makes Foued happy. His thing is to speak French in front of the cousins who don't understand it at all, the poor things, and to drive them especially crazy by teaching them a little slang. So then I hear Aunt Norah's little ones playing in the courtyard singing at the top of their lungs: "Fuck the po-po, fuck the po-po."

I talk about my cousin from Aïn Témouchent who asked for my hand after three days here. His name is Bilel, and it's like he's the sex symbol in the village, a real G, as Foued says. He has blue eyes and that's his trademark around here. All the honeys in this *bled* want him for a husband just for his beautiful eyes. He comes to Dar Mounia every day to see me, he struts around, shows his stuff. He thinks he's impressing me but he forgets that I live in France, and that I just have to take the metro to see some blue eyes. If he keeps flossin', God is going to punish his arrogance, and one morning without knowing how, he will wake up with brown eyes. And they'll be the most common brown in the world. That will teach him.

They've even vaguely talked to me about marriages of convenience they would have for me. Guys offering unbelievable sums to marry a girl with a CIF, a French identity card, the bids go up to seven thousand euros. I wonder where they find all this dough, it's alarming to see what they're ready to pay to know the other side.

The sardine vendor passes in front of me on his moped. The noise of the motor distracts me. It sounds weak, he should train with Speed Pizza—there, if your order doesn't arrive in half an hour, the pizza is free, so they're mostly interested in moving it fast. It's funny how life unwinds in slow motion here. Even if we haven't been there for a long time, Paris and its restlessness seem far away already. I get the feeling that my little brother would like to be there, but I hope that he understands too that his life isn't here in the *bled* and that he'll calm down when he gets back, because his expulsions worry me more and more. I think about them nonstop, even here. I dwell on the Tonislav story in every sense, I realize every day that those fuckheads aborted my love story and didn't give a shit about lighting up this poor guy's straw dreams. And then they think they're going to take my little brother?

Finally we leave for the post office in the city. We enter a huge room, armored by rows of phone booths, smothered by a hellish brouhaha, flooded by a whirlpool of djellabas and haiks. I would like to just call Auntie Mariatou to reassure her and to get some news of her little ones. So we go to the VIP corner, reserved for international calls, and there I see the fate of those who are brought here to disappear, to serve their second sentence. Their expression is the same as the one worn by the brothers I cross early in the morning at Saint-Lazare station, the ones who are cold and who walk with lowered heads. Crammed around these booths, these guys, as French as Foued or me, hold their handsets nervously, and watch the meter with anxiety. Sometimes they want to buy just a little more time, they scratch the bottom of their pockets to put in one last coin—they always say it's the last one . . . They call their mothers, their boys, maybe their girlfriends, they try to talk loud to cover the noise and I get the feeling that they actually

151

try just to talk at all. I explain all this to Foued, he watches them and I think he's as overwhelmed as I am. When we get back into Uncle Mohamed's car, no one says a word. We stay quiet all the way to the cemetery.

The rusty gate is wide open. The whiteness of the place hits me first, and its reach. It's striking.

But the most frightening is the birth dates, too recent, all the rows of tombs, these stars with five points looking east. It's hard to think about, but there are children under there. I realize then that Foued and me, we could have been buried here. That doesn't add up to much really. There were two hundred deaths that night, so two more . . .

The Boss is crouched down in front of the tomb, silent, stroking the ends of the white stone fingers. From time to time a sigh escapes from him and you would think that he understands everything, that he knows. I'm convinced that at this very moment he is all back in his head.

Foued stays standing, his eyes lowered, I hear him sniffling but I don't dare look at him to see if he's crying.

And me, I'm sitting on the same red earth, my palms flat on the ground, as if I wanted her to give me strength, the courage to leave again and face life.

We've prepared a prayer for her, for the others who rest here, and also for those who mourn them, for us, for the ones from over there. We will make a *sadaqa* in her memory this afternoon at the mosque.

·   ·   ·

Time doesn't work the same in Algeria, the hour of our departure sneaks up on us. I promise to come back very soon and not to forget. There are some things in this *bled* that I wouldn't find anywhere else. The atmosphere is strange, the odor is too and it's especially hot, maybe too hot. After all, it's only a question of climate and the Algerian heat anesthetized me.

Foued wants to stay a couple more days with The Boss. We work out the tickets so they can postpone their return. Me, I have to get back because Uncle Abdou put his foot down and he's waiting for me at the store.

Truce

I'M TKOed, I busted my body all night on the dance floor at
the Tropical Club, it was blazing thanks to the talents of deejay Patrick-Romuald. I'm taking advantage of my time alone.
I still have a week of liberty before Foued and The Boss come
back. I have the apartment all to myself.

Yesterday evening with Linda and Nawel, we really let
ourselves go. They managed to escape their boys, Issam and
Mouss. It was easy, there was a soccer match on TV.

We spent the evening with some Brazilian dancers, Coco,
Miguel, and Sadio. They had real class. Three handsome guys
who danced mad well. They taught us two or three steps and

bought us two or three fruit cocktails. Coco, the finest of the three, followed me the whole night and it was pretty nice. We danced all freaky and tight, glued together, sweating. It was exquisite.

Around four o'clock in the morning, me and Coco decided to leave the Tropical Club. The others wanted to stay. In the lobby while we were getting our stuff the girls gave me the thumbs-up and winked at me from afar. It was embarrassing.

Coco told me about another party nearby. The boy seemed like he was high, he seemed like he was built to go all night. We climbed into his Golf and it was like it was all custom made for him: the cream-colored leather seats, the Marvin Gaye CD in the stereo, the smooth ride . . . It's the Coco way. During the drive, he put his hand on my knee, smiled at me, and asked me in a suave voice if everything was cool.

We finally arrive. He parks the car and gives me a sweet, polite kiss. From here I can see the line. There are a hundred people. I'm too lazy to deal with that whole line. In the end we're not even guaranteed to get in. And now my feet hurt, I'm wearing shoes from the store. I have to remember that I spend my days selling low-quality shoes. Uncle Abdou's a crook after all.

Getting out of the car with Coco, I hear the birds. I hate hearing morning birds.

Coco waves to me and moves away. It's nice of him to drop me off. He seemed disappointed that I wasn't going with him to his party. He promised to call me tomorrow, but if he doesn't, it's no big thing for me. As Auntie often says: "You have to kiss a lot of toads before you can find your prince."

I move toward the line. Always the same tired faces. These weary people. Strangers, foreigners, who come at dawn for a ticket.

It's six o'clock in the morning and I'm in front of the prefecture.